# American Smile

**Also by Cody Young**

*Scandal at the Farmhouse*

For more information about this author visit:

**Codyyoungblog.blogspot.com**

# American
# Smile

Cody Young

**Golden Bay Press**

Golden Bay Press, Auckland, N.Z.

This is a work of fiction. Names, Characters, places and incidents are either the product of the author's imagination or are used fictitiously. Any resemblance to actual persons, living or dead, organizations, events or locales is entirely coincidental.

ISBN 978-0-473-15832-3

Printed in the United States of America.

National Library of New Zealand Cataloguing in Publication data:
Young, Cody.
American smile / by Cody Young.
ISBN 978-0-47315832-3
I. Title.
NZ823.3—dc 22

## Acknowledgements

*Thank you, Andrew, for giving me a real life love story.*

# 1

## American Smile

The secret came to the surface the year that Emma decided to keep her hair long. All winter she had let it grow and it was long and glossy down her back. It seemed a shame to cut it. So she broke the habit of a lifetime and left it long. That was the start of it all.

'I hope it's a great night,' Emma said, as they stood in the queue for the dance party.

'It had better be,' her friend Helen replied, preoccupied with sending a text. After a moment, she flipped her cell phone shut and started scanning the queue for interesting people. 'A group of guys from the Air Base are supposed to be coming. Real men for us to dance with. *American men.*'

They laughed but they were both nervous.

'Do I look all right?' Emma smoothed a strand of long dark hair back behind her ear, and turned to Helen for reassurance. 'Maybe I *should* have cut my hair. Mum says I look like a flower power girl.'

'What's wrong with that?'

'She thinks I should go to that place where she has hers done. Get it smartened up.'

'Don't! Long straight hair is a good modern look,' Helen said, 'Emma, with your dark hair and that red dress you're wearing, you look like a million dollars! Your mother is a fine woman in many ways, but her hair is like one of those wire things you scour out saucepans with. Promise me—swear to me—you'll never do that to your lovely hair!'

Emma smiled gratefully at her friend. 'Ok. The hippy look stays, for now.'

'I should think so. How old are you, now? Twenty-one, twenty-two? Old enough to ignore your mother, that's for sure. She can talk—I thought you said she was a real 'peace n love' type in her younger days!'

'She was.'

'Well, I wouldn't mention that to the guys in the armed forces. If you get talking to one of them, just act like you can't get enough of his tales of valour and victory!' Helen checked her lipstick, one more time. 'Let him think he's making a conquest.'

Emma glanced away. 'I'm here for the dancing.'

'No, you're not. I know you want to meet someone.'

Emma couldn't deny it. She knew it when she decided to wear her red halter-neck dress. Tonight, she wanted to be noticed. She was so jittery she began to wonder why she'd agreed to put herself through this, but in the sleepy English town where she lived there weren't many other opportunities. She'd been thrilled to hear there was a dance party on Saturday night. People were coming from far and wide, and it seemed like a chance not to be missed. Lots of new faces. Plenty of guys. Dancing til midnight.

Now they were here, she wasn't so sure. It wasn't at all what they'd been expecting. With a sense of crashing embarrassment, the young women soon realised they'd stumbled into some kind of partner-dancing event.

'The ad said *dance party*, didn't it?' Emma looked around the hall in surprise, and it did not look promising. They were early, which didn't help. The lights had not been dimmed and the hall was bright and bare. The organisers hadn't quite finished putting up the balloons. The DJ was still testing the amplifiers, and a handful of people were warming up, over by some seriously out-of-date audio equipment.

'Uh-huh.' Helen was equally dismayed. 'So where are the strobe lights and the techno music?'

'And the cool guys in the loose white singlets?' Emma said.

'And the alcohol,' Helen added crisply, 'because if they haven't got any of that, I'm definitely going home.'

So far, the only sign of any refreshment was an old trestle table with some plates of food covered in cling film. Uninspiring sandwiches and cheese sticks.

Helen was ready to bolt. 'Look, I'm sorry about this, I should have sussed it out properly. It's not really our scene is it? I didn't realise it was *partner* dancing.' She pulled at Emma's elbow and indicated that they should make a speedy escape.

Emma was reluctant to head for the door just yet. 'Why don't we stay and give it a try? We're all dressed up tonight, with nowhere else to go. There are people our age here, and more keep arriving. I like dancing, and it might be a laugh.'

'But I can't do all that old-fashioned stuff. I've got two left feet,' Helen protested.

'You've got a good sense of rhythm—you'll be fine. They say you shouldn't think about your feet. If someone asks you to dance, just remember: he leads, and you follow. Let's not go home. Not yet.'

At that moment, a man hauled up a metal grille and announced that the bar was open.

Helen turned like a homing pigeon towards it. 'Buy me a drink and I'll consider it. Make it a double, one for each of my two left feet,' she said, and then she sighed. 'I hope this isn't a BIG mistake.'

Emma laughed and said she'd get the first round, 'and then I vote we pretend to read the noticeboard, ok? Just until a few more people arrive. Let's reserve judgement until later.'

The queue for door sales was long, and the organisers seemed to expect a crowd. As soon as the music went on, the experienced dancers began whirling around the floor—enjoying the luxury of plenty of dance space. Although 'aerial' moves were banned by various bossy notices around the hall, a number of fast and furious manoeuvres took place. Emma watched the experienced dancers and envied their audacity and skill. The girls' skirts flew as the men twirled them around, and they made all the drops and laybacks look so easy.

'Do you do the French Jive?' said a voice beside her elbow.

Emma didn't get the chance to say yes or no. She found herself in the arms of a short but very determined Polish guy who wanted to try all sorts of moves she didn't know. After that there was a heavy-looking bank manager who lurched her around the floor as if she was a sack of potatoes. There was a man who asked her if she spoke English. Emma taught that subject at school so she told him she could get by. The final humiliation was the man who stood on her shoe. Unfortunately, the toe of his boot landed on the edge of her open sandal just at the same instant that Emma was trying to move her foot in the opposite direction. The dainty little strap broke and she was forced to limp off the dance floor.

Emma took off her shoe and inspected the damage. The ankle strap was ripped away from the rest of the shoe. There didn't seem to be much she could do to salvage it.

Helen came over, when she realised her friend had become an early casualty. She took a good look at the shoe. 'I don't suppose you brought a spare pair?'

'Of course not.'

They'd only been at the dance for twenty minutes. Emma sighed. What kind of an evening could she have with a broken shoe? She supposed she'd have to resign herself to being a wallflower.

'Do you want me to ask around? Loads of people change into special shoes when they get here—maybe someone would lend you their ordinary pair.'

'I don't know, Helen, it's a bit embarrassing to ask a total stranger to give me their shoes—and I'd have to find someone the right size.'

'I'm just trying to come up with a practical solution.'

'I think I'll just watch for a while, ok?'

* * *

At the dance, a pair of young men stood by the soft drinks machine—a great place to start conversations. One was dark and one was fair. They had close cropped hair and neatly pressed shirts. Both men were a little taller than average, and they had that well-groomed, well-fed look that immediately gave the clue to where they were from. The fair-haired guy spoke first.

'Hey Tyler, you got the money for the next round? I'll stay here and guard our position.'

'Everything is tactics to you, huh?' Tyler smiled and felt in his pocket for his wallet. Then he frowned. 'Are you just trying to get me out of your way?'

'All's fair in love and war.'

Tyler didn't move. He didn't want a drink as much as he wanted a girl. They both scanned the room, yet again. New people kept arriving. The atmosphere was heating up. The blond guy—Bradley—seemed to notice every second girl. Tyler noticed only one—the luscious one in the red dress. He tried to play it cool. He frowned into his empty beer glass, and wondered what he should do next.

'Check out that one over there! A six out of ten, maybe even a seven,' said Bradley, and he gave his friend a nudge. Tyler hoped he didn't mean the girl in red.

'Would you keep your voice down? How would you like it, if she gave *you* marks outta ten?'

'Don't get all uptight on me, buddy. I don't have to spend my Saturday night in a place like this, you know,' Brad gave a supercilious glance around the room, until his gaze fell on a couple of newcomers. 'Hey, look at those two, just coming through the door! They're not so bad. Which one do you like, Tyler—the blonde, or the redhead?'

Tyler nodded his head in the opposite direction. On the other side of the hall, by a door marked 'fire exit', the young woman in the red dress was trying to decide what to do about her broken shoe.

'The girl with the long hair—that's the one I like.'

\* \* \*

'May I have the pleasure?' he asked.

'What?' Emma looked up at the young man. It was such an archaic phrase. It matched his conservative clothing and his Air Force haircut.

'Of this dance,' he added, by way of clarification. He was standing with his hand held out towards her.

She liked the way he said 'dance'. *Very American.* 'I don't know,' she said, with an apologetic grin, 'the strap has come off my shoe.'

'Yeah, I saw,' he said.

That made her feel awkward. He'd probably seen the whole performance with the other men. She hesitated, and he looked a bit crestfallen.

'Would it be ok to dance in bare feet, do you think?' she said.

'I could try to steer us away from the crowd,' he offered, 'so people don't stamp on your toes. I could even take my own shoes off, if you like.'

He was so polite and so hopeful.

'Ok,' she said. She tossed her shoes over by the wall, and he loosened his lace-ups and kicked them off too. She hoped he wouldn't slip over in his grey socks.

Then they turned back to face each other. He broke into a big dimply smile and took her hand. He led her onto the dance floor. He told her his name was Tyler, but she didn't manage to reply—she was too busy concentrating on the dance steps.

6

Some people are a dream to dance with, and others—not so good. Emma was a little nervous after the nightmare dance with the guy who wrecked her shoe, but fortunately Tyler was a good dancer. His lead was strong enough to make her feel that he was in command, but not so domineering and pushy that she felt manhandled all the time. A girl likes to be twirled around a bit. A clever dancer knows when to let his partner enjoy a spin and when to surprise her with a close seductive move.

Emma liked the way this guy pulled her in and held her tight. They seemed to fit together perfectly. She liked the strength in his arms when he caught her at the end of a spin, and she liked the sparkle in his eyes when she looked up at him. And when he led her into an unexpected embrace, it was sheer delight.

At the end of the third song, he said he wanted to buy her a drink. Her feet hurt and she needed a rest, but she wasn't so keen on this part. One minute they were dancing in an intimate, physical kind of way, the next they were back to polite enquiries about places of work and the weather.

He asked her name, and she told him.

'Emma,' he said, and he smiled. 'That's just lovely—and it suits you, too. Is it like the girl in that book by Jane Austen?' The funny way he said 'Austen' made her smile too.

'There are lots of Emmas. You meet them everywhere,' she said with a shrug. 'It's just an ordinary name.'

'You're not ordinary. There's no one else here like you,' he said and then he frowned, as if he hadn't meant to say what he was thinking. He coloured up and asked her about what she did in her free time. She told him she did some swimming. He said he played the guitar.

Bradley lurched up with beery breath, and commented that Emma really seemed to know how to shake what her momma gave her. Tyler apologized for his crass friend, and hissed in Bradley's ear.

'Please! We don't want to get ourselves a reputation.'

Helen came and asked the guys about the U.S. Air Force. She wanted to know if either of them was a pilot. A tactless enquiry, Emma thought.

'Sorry to disappoint you,' Tyler said, 'you'll be lucky to meet a pilot these days; our operations here in Britain have been scaled right back, and for each person who gets to fly there are about a hundred on the ground. I'm an aircraft mechanic. So is Brad.'

'Different specialties, though.' Bradley said, letting his arm slide along the bar behind Helen's back. 'It's a very specialised occupation.'

'So what does it involve?' Emma asked, but only to be polite.

Bradley began to describe his 'specialty' in terms of heavy innuendo. 'Oh, strippin' her down, checking all moving parts, makin' her go, makin' her purr...'

Helen grinned. Tyler turned his head away.

'What about you?' Emma said, meaning Tyler, but he was looking in the other direction and he didn't reply.

'He can do some of that stuff too, if anyone ever asks him,' Bradley said.

*Why wouldn't they*, Emma thought to herself, looking at Tyler. *He's absolutely gorgeous.*

It was as if he heard what she was thinking, because Tyler turned and glanced at her and his hazel eyes met hers. He smiled as if they had known each other since way back when. Then he blushed and stared into his beer glass.

Tyler was nervous, but he didn't think he was doing too bad, if the look in this girl's eyes was saying what he thought it was saying. Bradley and Helen danced some more, which was a mercy, and Tyler made use of the time by getting to know his quarry. 'You've got links with the United States yourself?' he said, leaning closer to Emma to make himself heard over the dance music.

'No, not really,' she said with a laugh. 'What on earth makes you say that?'

'Don't you have relatives over there?' he said pleasantly.

'No, none at all,' she said, 'my family has lived in Devon since time began. We've traced seven generations of us, in the records, and our roots here go back a lot further than that, I should think.'

'My mistake. I just thought—looking at you—that you might be-' Just before it was too late, Tyler decided it would be best if he didn't say it. He had often been told that tact wasn't his greatest gift.

She frowned. 'Looking at me you thought what?'

'I'm sorry. Maybe I've had a little too much to drink. The last thing I meant to infer was any… comment… that might be seen as… inappropriate.'

'What are you talking about?' she looked completely confused by that last remark.

'I didn't mean to offend you, I really didn't -'

'I'm not offended,' she said, 'why should I be?'

'Please forget my ramblings. It must be the liquor.' It wasn't. This girl had a certain look about her that he had seen before. He knew his chat up line had stalled and had gone into a nosedive. It looked like it was about to crash and burn on frostbitten fields below. In order to salvage something from the final descent, Tyler clutched at the first thing he could think of to say to her that she might like to hear.

'You've got an American smile, that's all I meant.'

'Oh. Really? I'll take that as a compliment!'

'That's how I meant it,' he said, apologetically.

Emma felt awkward, and turned away from him. She caught sight of herself in the glass door panel, and she frowned. An American smile, indeed! She knew she wasn't exactly a Hollywood 'it' girl. He was a slightly odd young man, Tyler. She began to wonder if she should go and look for another guy to dance with. Trouble was, she hadn't seen anyone else as good-looking as this one.

Helen came blundering through the crowd, and hauled Emma into the corridor. Helen said she was sick of the party and wanted to go home. Bradley had made a suggestion on the veranda that she had found quite offensive. She would not say exactly what it was, but it seemed to have put Helen off Americans for the time being.

'I should have slapped his face,' she said.

'Gosh, I'm glad you didn't. We'd be barred from here if you did anything like that!'

'Who cares? I don't think I want to come here again, anyway.'

'No, but I might,' Emma said. She hadn't even got the chance to say goodnight to the young mechanic.

'Come off it, Emma. I can't exactly see you with a military man.'

'That's not what you said earlier. You said it would be great to meet some guys from the base.'

Helen scowled. She wanted to go home, and she wanted to go now. She looked a bit angry and red in the face. She was in no fit state to drive anywhere. Emma decided she'd better get her friend out of the dancehall and away from Brad before anything else went wrong. She knew Helen would do the same for her. Besides, she had to get up early to teach the Swim Squad tomorrow morning. She went to look for her shoes.

* * *

Emma was staying at her parents' place, just for now, just until she got herself together again. She let herself into the cottage, and was surprised to hear voices coming from the kitchen. Her parents didn't wait up for her these days.

She found them sitting at the kitchen table in front of a pot of tea. Her mother was in tears, and her father was holding her hand.

'What's happened?'

Keith Rowland, Emma's dad, looked up. 'We've had a phone call from The Willows, sweetie.' Emma's grandparents lived in sheltered accommodation on the other side of town.

'Is Grandpa George, ok?' Emma was kind of expecting this. They all knew that George had a weak heart, and he'd already had a scare last year.

Keith nodded. 'Yes, he's flustered and upset, but he's fine. It's your Grandma that's gone.'

'No!'

Emma's mother Susan dabbed at her face with a tissue and tried to explain. 'She didn't suffer, she just slipped away,' she said. 'But the nurse I spoke to said that she kept saying something about *burning the letters*.'

'What letters?' asked Emma, sitting down at the table.

'I have no idea. I'd ask your grandfather but I'm not sure if I should upset him at a time like this. They were married for nearly seventy years. He'll be lost without her.'

Emma was curious now. 'Not letters from Grandpa George, surely? She wouldn't want to burn those.'

Susan shook her head. 'I can't think of *any* kind of letter that she'd need to burn. She never had any secrets. Not from me.'

# 2

# The Swimming Pool

Emma never dreamt he'd come looking for her. On Sunday morning she always took the Junior Swim Squad for their training session. Nobody else wanted to teach the Sunday morning class, but she liked it a lot. Her nine and ten year olds were always full of energy and it put her in a good mood for the rest of the day.

She didn't realise it was him at first. There was a man ploughing up and down in the 'medium' lane, doing a strong overarm crawl, but all she saw was good technique. She was busy with the little girls. The minute they were allowed to, the girls all dived off the side into the water and began swimming about like a shoal of sardines. Emma had a whistle she could blow if she wanted to get their attention, but for now she let them go wild. They'd do some serious swimming when everyone had got the silliness out of their systems.

Out of the corner of her eye she saw him pull himself out of the water, and walk towards her. Water was dripping off his body, and his navy blue board shorts clung to his legs. He was wearing goggles. He walked right up to her.

'Emma!'

She only realised it was him when he took the goggles off. They left red imprints around his eyes and over his nose.

'Tyler Robinson,' he said, 'from the dance, last night.' He tried to shake her hand, which seemed a very odd thing to do when he was all wet, and they were standing beside a swimming pool, half-naked.

'Oh, hi!' she said. 'It's you.'

'Yup. Me,' he said.

'Sorry. You look different,' she said, trying not to look at his chest or anything, '—with your hair wet.'

'Do I?' he said, and the dimpled smile came back. She remembered that smile. *He* was the one with the American smile.

He glanced down at his bare feet. 'You did mention that you came here on Sunday mornings. I wondered if it was just part of the brush off, but I was hoping it was true. I've been here since 7 a.m. to make sure I didn't miss you. I thought you said it was early!'

'Ten o'clock is early. Especially if you've been to a party the night before. Why ever did you hang around all that time?'

'The obvious reason. I wanted to see you again. And I wanted to apologise for any comment I may have made under the influence of liquor. I feel kinda dumb about it.'

'Heavens, don't worry. It was nothing!' Emma wasn't even sure *what* it was, but obviously Tyler was a bit sensitive about it. The embarrassment was fairly intense for both of them, just at that moment. The swimming pool wasn't a great place for an early encounter. Emma wished she was wearing more clothes, for a start. It seemed weird to be having such an odd conversation with a man she liked but hardly knew at all. It was unfortunate that she'd ended up in her second best swimsuit; the better one was in the wash. At least her legs were nice and brown.

'Have you really been here since seven?' she asked, at a loss to know what else to say.

'I shouldn't have told you that,' he said, grinning at her, 'that was kinda dumb too.'

'I have to teach the squad,' she said. 'We're preparing for a competition.'

'Of course. Great squad. Full of enthusiasm,' he said. 'Emma?'

'Yes?'

'May I wait?' he asked, 'and talk to you afterwards? Would that be ok? Please tell me if I'm intruding.'

She wondered if he was always so polite. 'I don't mind if you stay,' she said. 'Maybe you can help us out. Can you use a stopwatch?'

'Of course I can. I wanted to offer to help,' he said, glancing in the direction of the kids. 'But with them all being, um... *young ladies*, I was worried it might not be appropriate.'

Tyler seemed to worry a lot about what was 'appropriate', but Emma didn't have time to ask him about that now. She just handed him the stopwatch and went to get the girls to line up along the edge of the pool. She jumped into the water, and they all giggled because she made a splash.

'Come on girls! Let's start with our favourite—the butterfly stroke! Mr Robinson is going to time us today, so we'll have to swim extra fast to impress him.'

\* \* \*

Afterwards they met up again in the vestibule. He looked all clean and wholesome in a light blue sweatshirt with the sleeves pushed up. His dark hair was still wet but neatly combed. His swimming kit was in a sports bag at his feet. It had a US air force badge on the side.

'Mustn't forget to return your stopwatch,' he said, as he got it out of his pocket and placed it in her hand. He had hazel eyes. Nice eyes, with just a hint of worried uncertainty in them. He was nervous. He was trying to hide it though.

'Thank you,' Emma said, and put the watch in her handbag. 'It was great to have a second person to help out.'

'Yeah,' he said, 'it's brave of you to do this all on your own.'

'I enjoy it.' She smiled and turned to go. The moment to say goodbye had come, and she wasn't sure what was in the script. Some of the girls were already waiting for their parents on the front steps just outside.

'I'd like the opportunity to—' he began.

'Miss Rowland! Gillian's left her towel in the changing rooms!'

'Ok, sweetie, just go up to the desk and explain. They'll let her go back in and get it.'

Tyler started again. 'I sure would like the chance to –'

'Miss! Miss! Have you got change for the coke machine? Please, Miss Rowland?'

'Here. Take this.' Tyler handed her a coin.

'Oh no, Tyler, you mustn't. Give that back to Mr Robinson, there's a good girl. We don't accept money from strangers, do we?'

'But I want a coke. I NEED one. And I do know Mr Robinson. He's your friend, isn't he?'

'Really, I'm happy to, Emma. I was just hoping to get a chance to—'

A precocious little miss in a halter neck top spoke up at that point. 'Mr Robinson? Are you going to ask Miss Rowland out, maybe?'

Tyler was taken aback for a second, but then he grinned at the little lady. 'Well, Yes! Yes, I am. Thank you for helping me out,' he said. 'Emma, can you meet me Saturday? Maybe about two?'

Loads of laughter. Little girls on all sides, holding on to Emma's hands, her skirts, and her bag. Lots of expectant faces looking up at Tyler.

'Are you going to say YES, Miss Rowland?'

'Well...'

'He's *nice*, Miss. You should say yes.'

'Can I have the money for my coke now, Miss?'

'Um... ok,' she said, 'I mean, maybe I've got some change here...'

Tyler decided to act as if she'd said yes to his proposal. 'I'll meet you at the ice cream stand on the pier. The one with the big cone kinda stickin' out of the top at a forty-five degree angle.'

'What?' she said.

'I can show you where that is, Miss Rowland. I know that place!'

Tyler smiled at the little girl who said that.

'I know where it is,' Emma said, still searching in her bag so she didn't have to look at Tyler.

'Great,' he said. 'Come alone. No offence intended and all, but come alone.' He made sure he got her number this time, too.

What was she thinking! Arranging to meet a man for ice creams on the promenade. She was forgetting that her grandmother had just passed away. Her mother was in a complete state, and they were in the middle of making all the arrangements for the funeral. All that had gone out of her head when Tyler turned up.

# 3

## Soldier Boys

**March 1944**

It was midday and it was almost warm and sunny. The deck of the troopship was crowded with American servicemen. No one wanted to be down below when they could be out here among friends, gazing out across the sparkling water. Everybody was smoking cigarettes and laughing at the slightest hint of a joke. You'd think from all the banter they were going on a cruise. It had been like that all the way from New York.

There was a lot of speculation about their destination, which was, like so many things, a secret. One guy said he thought he'd seen the coast of Ireland, and he could well have been right—everyone believed they were headed for Britain.

Standing on the deck in his new uniform, Joe listened to all the talk and smiled to himself. He loved the way the guys kept calling it 'the European Theater'—like there would be plush seats and pretty girls selling ice cream and wafers. He had to keep reminding himself that they meant the theater of war.

Later, every soldier was given a pamphlet about how to behave in the company of English people, and the mystery was solved. They'd be stationed in Britain, to wait for the order to go and fight in France.

As they came into port they caught glimpses of the city, and everyone jostled forward to try and get a look at the place. Joe had never seen anything like it. He was from a little one-horse town and this was like nothing on earth to him. The bomb damage, the grime, the little houses all hunched up together like they were feeling the cold. Some buildings were blackened by fire, or that's what it looked like, but maybe it was just dirt.

'Is it London?' someone asked.

'No, it's Liverpool.'

The ship had an English crew, and one of the sailors warned the men that they wouldn't feel at home when they went on shore. 'You people always say our tea's like dirty water and our coffee tastes like mud,' he said, and he laughed and lit up a smoke. 'Nothing like a British cuppa, in my opinion, of course. You might get to like it. Don't expect ham and eggs for breakfast, though, and don't go stealing our girls!'

Joe and his new buddies didn't care. There was a holiday atmosphere on the troopship and nothing could spoil it. They were ready to take the place as they found it, and they were looking forward to meeting the natives. There was a frenzy of activity around the man selling bars of chocolate, as it was widely believed that candy was the best way to make themselves popular when they got off the boat.

Joe glanced through his little book of instructions for mixing with the Brits. Don't brag. Don't be rude about the food, or lack of it. Don't expect hot showers and clean towels. There's a war on, and everyone is pitching in. You may even find you have to take orders from a woman.

Women. Joe ran a hand through his slick dark hair and took stock of his chances of impressing the girls. He was a good-looking guy, and he knew it. He was wearing the finest suit of clothes he'd ever possessed, courtesy of the U.S. Army. But back home he wasn't anybody. No education, to speak of. He didn't exactly have a way with words, either...

As the gangplank went down, Joe shouldered his heavy pack and joined the long line of men waiting to disembark. He made his way down the gangway toward the quayside, feeling the gangplank flex under his step.

Joe knew that he was a little apprehensive, now that the time came to leave the ship. He stepped onto the concrete wharf and joined the surging crowd of soldiers. Who could tell what he'd find in this unfamiliar place, and how long it would be before he saw some action. He tried not to think of home, and his chances of seeing it again.

He followed the horde over to an area 'manned' by the Red Cross, where he was greeted by a matronly lady in an enormous tea-stained apron. She was very posh, he could tell.

'Welcome to Britain,' she said, automatically, and handed him a cup of boiling hot, bright orange tea. 'You're such brave boys, every one of you.'

Joe laughed. She didn't even know what the word meant, not to him. 'Thank you ma'am,' he said, and touched his cap.

# 4

## Grandma's Little Secret

The ceremony was quiet and dignified. On a sunny Wednesday afternoon they said their goodbyes to Grandma Evelyn in the parish church. They sang a couple of hymns and played a lovely piece of music from Faure's Requiem. There was a nice big wreath in the shape of an 'E' and lots of other floral tributes, including a great many lilies, Evelyn's favourite flower.

Emma's father gave a beautiful eloquent speech, and if he had any thoughts at all about his mother-in-law's flaws, he kept them to himself. He focused on what a marvellous person Evelyn had been, and how much his wife Susan had loved her mother and wanted to be like her. He didn't say that he was glad that she wasn't. He told them how proud Evelyn had been the night that Emma was born, and how much she enjoyed being a glamorous granny. He never said a word about her dubious choice of birthday gifts or the way she used to lay down the law about how Emma should be brought up.

Afterwards, everyone went over to the Horse and Plough for a ham sandwich and a pint of beer. People were subdued, but friendly, as they hugged one another and reminisced about Evelyn's younger days. It was nice that so many people had been able to get the time off to come to the funeral; Emma saw some faces she hadn't seen for years, including a cousin she hadn't set eyes on since she was four. She stood at her parents' side and everyone said what a credit she was to them.

It was all going smoothly until one of Emma's aunts cornered her over by the refreshments.

'What a shame your young man couldn't come, Emma,' she announced.

*Trust Aunt Meg not to be up to speed with recent events*, Emma thought, dreading having to explain that she no longer had 'a young man'. She couldn't escape, though.

'Actually, Matthew and I aren't seeing each other any more.'

'Oh no! He was *lovely*, Emma. Such a great sense of humour and so very attractive—'

Susan Rowland moved swiftly to rescue her daughter. 'It was not to be. Emma's met someone new, Meg.'

Emma squirmed. She hadn't exactly got very far up the primrose path with Tyler. Not even a first date at this stage.

'Someone new?' Aunt Meg said, turning on poor Emma. 'Why would you want someone new when you were with a wonderful man like Matthew? What went wrong? Didn't you try to work things out, dear?'

Emma couldn't even begin to reply.

'Don't let's dwell on the past, Meg. I'm sure Emma's new fellow is very nice too. He's in the Air Force, isn't he?' Susan smiled a message to her daughter. *Be brave, don't cry, keep your chin up.*

'Yes.' Emma stared very hard at a plate of asparagus rolls on the buffet table, trying to will herself to stay upbeat and dry-eyed. 'But I hardly know him—'

'The Air Force? Well, there's your first problem.'

'Meg!' Susan said, with a meaningful scowl.

'I can't see a member of the armed forces fitting in with Our Family,' Meg said, as if she was talking about the inhabitants of Balmoral Castle. 'Heavens, Emma, your Grandpa George was a conscientious objector!'

21

'Was he, Mum? Was Grandpa a conchie?' Emma asked—any topic of conversation was better than thinking about Matthew. Besides, it was the first she'd heard of it.

'Yes dear—he did play his part in World War Two, though. He was in bomb disposal.'

Grandpa George turned around when he heard that, ignoring various people who were trying to offer their sympathies. 'What's all this about Grandpa?' he said, and he limped a few paces towards them with the aid of his old wooden walking stick. 'Did I hear you talking about me and my wartime exploits?'

'Yes, Dad. Come and tell us all about it. Bomb disposal, wasn't it? We've got a situation right here that needs defusing,' Susan said, with another tense smile. 'Tell us about that time when you weren't sure which of the wires to cut first!'

Emma smiled. Her mother was a born peacemaker, in every sense of the word. It was nice to be among family and friends again. Even on a sad day like this. She was so glad to be back in Devon, where she belonged. Last year, when she was fresh out of teacher's college she had taken a job in Manchester, and it had not been a happy experience. A big unfamiliar city, a rough school, and some cold, shabby lodgings. 'And you went and got your heart broken,' her father used to say—as if it was Emma's fault. It had been a tough year, but it was worth it because it helped her get the job back home. It was lovely to be in the little seaside town where she grew up, surrounded by people who cared about her. Even so, Emma was thankful when the day was over.

'Did you get a chance to ask anyone about the letters, Mum?' Emma wanted to know, when the last person had gone and the farewells were over.

'No, but I'm clearing out her stuff next week. I'll keep a sharp eye out for them.'

* * *

Emma's mother prided herself on her capacity to keep busy even in times of sadness. With the funeral over, Susan simply dried her eyes and got on with it all. She was a powerhouse of efficiency.

By Friday morning, Susan was at The Willows helping Grandpa George sort out Evelyn's things, which some of the other residents thought was rather hasty. Susan claimed that she just wanted it done. She began the task of tidying up everything that Evelyn had left behind—her papers and unpaid bills and magazine subscriptions. Susan knew she'd feel a lot better when it was all in order.

Before long, Susan moved on to the next task and got all her mother's clothes bagged up for the charity shop—and she didn't shed a single tear—even though she'd been ever so fond of her mother. After she'd dealt with the wardrobe she started pulling out stuff from under the bed—an old hatbox stuffed with receipts, pots of dried up shoe cream, and an ancient sports bag with some pre-war ice-skates inside.

'These should be in a museum, look!'

Finally, she found a battered brown leather suitcase with reinforced corners. It was bulging with memorabilia and old papers. She dragged it through into the lounge, and started going through the contents.

Grandpa George hovered by the mantelpiece. 'I thought I burned those,' he said. He sounded vague and dithery. He frowned down at the papers his daughter was leafing through. 'I meant to put all that in the boiler.'

Susan sometimes wondered if his mind was starting to go. 'Don't worry, Dad. I'll sort it out. Some of it's quite interesting really. Oh look, mum's old passport from the 1950s. Would you look at that! Wasn't she gorgeous!'

George sighed and came doddering across the room to look.

'She was a fine looking woman, indeed she was. Let me sort out all of that, dear, I'm not helpless, you know.'

'I'll have it done in a few minutes, Dad. Don't fret! I won't throw away anything important, I promise.'

'Most of it needs to be thrown away. It's all in the past now.' He nearly knocked a little vase off the mantelpiece as he stood there, fidgeting, as if he was trying to decide what to do next. His daughter was just too efficient for her own good.

Susan was leafing through the papers, putting them in piles on the lounge carpet, dividing them into categories.

'These look semi-official, Dad, should they be in the safe, do you think?'

He ran a hand over his face in anxiety. 'Susie, don't. None of it is of any consequence. You give that here to me. I want to burn the lot of it.'

It was too late. Susan turned the page. She found herself reading some correspondence about a little girl that Evelyn and George were thinking of adopting. She read on, scanning the lines. She found it fascinating.

'I never knew you and mum tried to adopt,' she said, and she looked up from yellowing piece of paper on her lap. 'What a shame—I would have loved to have a sister. What happened? Why didn't it go through?'

There was a long, long pause. Susan had never seen such an extraordinary look on her father's face. He sat down in the chair opposite Susan. He reached out with old knotty fingers, to take her hands.

'It did go through, love.'

# 5

## The Family Tree

The Rowlands' cottage stood where it had always stood, on the main road that led down to the bay, in a pleasant seaside town on the South Coast of England. When it was first built it must have seen hay carts going by, and men and women on their way to market. Today, the road that passed the front door was busy with Saturday traffic. Lots of cars and lorries whizzed past the front door, ruffling the plants in the window boxes.

Inside the cottage, things were not calm and unruffled either. Yesterday, Susan had come home from The Willows in a state of great distress. Last night she had sobbed her eyes out about the whole adoption business and only managed to go to sleep with the aid of a warm drink and a sleeping pill.

Today, she had spent the morning trying to be brave and get on with things, but all the unanswered questions kept crowding her mind. Who were her real parents? Did they love each other? Why couldn't they keep her and raise her themselves? Why on earth did Evelyn and George try to hush it up and keep it all a secret?

In the neat little hallway, above the antique telephone table and the potted plant, there was a beautiful silver frame hanging on the wall. Susan stood staring at it now. Underneath the glass was a family tree. The names of Susan's forebears had all been neatly rendered in ink, in curly lettering. All the people seemed to be called John and Mary and William and Anne. A brightly coloured crest adorned the top. It had been a Christmas present from Susan's parents. The silver frame and the glass had been lovingly polished, once a week, for the last eight years.

'Lies!' Susan said, and on a mad impulse, she lifted the offensive object down from its hook on the wall. She vented her feelings by throwing it down her hallway in the direction of the kitchen door. Susan was a strong woman and she threw it with a good deal of violent passion, as if she was a champion of the shot put. The picture hit the door at considerable speed and smashed into a thousand pieces all over the immaculate hall carpet.

Then Susan put her head against the wall and cried her eyes out. The kitchen door creaked as Emma pushed it open to see if her mother was hurt. She surveyed the shattered wreckage of the family tree amongst the bits of broken glass on the floor.

'Should I get the dust buster out?' Emma asked tentatively, from just behind the doorframe.

'It's going to take a lot more than that, to clear up this almighty mess!' Susan screamed at her. She couldn't calm down. All the information about this person and that, all the people that she had thought she was related to, it was all LIES.

Keith Rowland came running in from the garden when he heard the noise, and he looked most dismayed when he saw what his wife had done to the family tree and the back of their kitchen door. He picked up the twisted silver frame, wondering if it could be repaired.

He could hardly credit it. Susan was normally such a sensible woman. She'd been a nurse before Emma was born—cheerful, hardworking, and marvellous in a crisis. She ran their house like a tight ship too—coping well with all the stresses and strains of being a wife and mother. Nothing ever seemed to get the better of her.

Now, here she was, collapsed in a tearful heap on the stairs, repeating the same phrase over and over again. 'I don't know who I am, any more. I don't know who I am.'

'Susan, love, you are my wife and Emma's mum. It doesn't matter in the slightest that you are adopted. It doesn't change anything.'

'It changes EVERYTHING,' Susan insisted, and burst into a fresh bout of sobbing. 'For a start, it has turned my parents—people I loved and trusted—into a pair of compulsive liars.'

Keith and Emma exchanged worried glances. In a way they really wished she hadn't found out. It must be hard for a woman of sixty-four to reconcile herself to that kind of news after spending her whole life trying to believe what Evelyn and George had wished was the truth.

'Don't blame silly old George, love,' Keith told her. 'I expect it was your mother's wish that you shouldn't be told. You know how devoted he was to her.'

'But what about ME, why didn't they think about the effect it would have on ME! My whole sense of identity was based on something that isn't true,' Susan said, trying to wipe the tears away with Keith's handkerchief. 'I liked to think of myself as 'a Devon woman', Keith.'

'I know.'

'I've been made a fool of. A complete idiot—and it's not just a private humiliation either. What are they going to think at the Genealogy Society? I really enjoyed belonging to that. Heavens, Keith, last year I gave that talk at the Women's Institute—about finding my great great grandparents, and tracing my family all the way back to 1332.'

Keith raised his eyebrows. He knew that Susan had been hoping to find evidence that took the family history right back to the time of the Domesday Book. 'You may have to make a few adjustments to the research you've done so far—'

'Adjustments! I asked Dad to tell me everything he knew and the only shred of information he could give me was that my real mother was 'some unfortunate little thing from London'—his

27

words, not mine. He couldn't tell me anything about 'the man'. Nothing is known about him. My father. He could have been anybody. All the research I've done so far is wrong. George and Evelyn sat back and let me do all that, knowing full well that it was based on lies, lies, lies.'

Susan was forced to reconcile herself to the fact that she probably wasn't related to anyone in Devon at all.

'You know, I really think they thought it was for the best if you didn't know,' Emma said suddenly. 'I think that's what people truly believed in the past.'

'They were wrong. I need to know the truth. The whole foundation on which I have built my identity is a lie. That family tree was a bloody lie—and the worst thing is that it was a lie that I was proud of! I have lived with it here in my hallway for the last eight years. I have shown it to all our friends and neighbours. I feel like such a fool! I have perpetuated some crazy idea of Evelyn's without any idea what actually happened. I'm glad I smashed it. I'm really glad.'

Susan blew her nose, and tried to compose herself. Suddenly, a flash of her old self returned, and she looked up at Emma as if she was discussing the nursing rosters. 'Darling, didn't you have an appointment or something, this afternoon?'

Emma had completely forgotten. 'Oh my goodness! Tyler! What time is it? Is it past two o'clock?'

\* \* \*

Emma didn't like daytime dates. They were a bit non-committal, a bit something and nothing. It was so much easier for a man to walk away from a cup of coffee than the full dinner deal. He could simply cut things short and pretend he was never really interested in the first place. All the same, a date was a date, and she hadn't meant to stand him up. She knew that if she was late he'd think she'd had second thoughts.

Everything was just a bit crazy at the moment. Maybe she should have told him there was too much going on at home and she would have to cancel. She had his number. One terse little text message and all her problems would be solved.

Emma didn't think she could do that to a guy who had travelled nearly thirty miles for an ice cream. The air base was the other side of Exeter.

There was no time to change or put her hair up, she just went as she was. She did not feel very alluring in her old blue t-shirt and a pair of cotton trousers that she usually did her chores in. None of that mattered as long as he was still there. She ran as fast as she could down to the seafront and then slowed down, trying very hard to look relaxed and nonchalant.

When she saw him waiting for her, she caught her breath. There he was, waiting to see her. Sunglasses, jeans, arms resting on the rail as he looked out to sea. He looked good in his clothes —that's for sure—and somehow, knowing what was underneath made him even more attractive. Her mind kept replaying the preview at the swimming pool. Today, he wore a dark navy shirt with short sleeves. He saw her and stood to attention as she approached. He waved and put his sunglasses in his top pocket. He didn't seem to mind that she was late.

'Hello!' she said, 'I like your shirt. That dark blue looks good on you.' She'd never been afraid to give a man a compliment. Besides, he was the one who had got dressed up.

'Thank you, Emma. I'm so glad you approve. I bought it today.' Then he blushed, as if he hadn't meant to admit that.

Emma just smiled and nodded, and asked him if he'd had a look through the pay-per-view binoculars.

He was very attentive about getting her the right ice cream, and paying for the binoculars, and he was most concerned when she told him about her grandmother. He said how sorry he was for her loss.

'It's ok. She was very old, and she'd lived a full life.' Emma was glad that Tyler didn't seem to mind her mentioning the bereavement.

'It's always sad to lose a loved one—even if it wasn't unexpected,' he said. His young face was full of sympathy and concern.

Then Emma found herself telling him about the part of it that *was* unexpected, including the smashed family tree. Tyler's eyebrows went up when she said that.

'High drama,' he said.

She instantly regretted what she'd said. He would get the wrong impression. He would think badly of her mum. 'Gosh, Tyler—please don't think we're all violent and bad-tempered. Mum is normally such a restrained, orderly sort of person. My dad couldn't believe it when she did that. I don't think she's broken so much as a teacup since 1975.'

Tyler smiled and the dimples appeared again. 'In that case she deserves to kick up a bit of a fuss. She's been the perfect daughter for all these years and now she's completely confused about who she really is.'

'Grandpa hasn't been all that helpful either. He said the only thing he knew was that the baby—my mum—was born to a young girl from London. That's the only piece of information he has.'

'That must be hard for your mom,' he said. 'You know, I'm sure there must be a lot more you could find out for her, if you wanted to.'

'I do want to. She's really upset. I'd like to help her.'

He hesitated, as if he wanted to speak, but he had to find the right words, 'I really think I could help you sort all this out, Emma.'

'Could you?'

'Yeah, I've got this feeling that—' Tyler paused. 'Look, all I'm trying to say is that I think I can help, if you would permit me to?'

Emma said that would be nice. Hell, she wasn't about to say no! Then a thought crossed her mind. 'Tyler, has this got anything to do with what you said at the dance? About the way I look?'

'Maybe. Let's not go into that now.'

'Did you mean that I look familiar?' she asked, her curiosity aroused. She wished he would say what he suspected—it might be important now that she knew her mother was adopted.

'Yeah… in a way. But let's not speculate until we get the facts, ok?'

She smiled, and they changed the subject, for now.

As they walked along the same stretch of promenade for the third time, Tyler explained that he had jumped at the chance of a 'Change of Station'. He said he was really excited to be in England with its history and all. He told her about everything the Department of Defence had done for him to make the relocation go smoothly. Tyler said they had programs for everything—seminars and stuff—about avoiding culture shock and adapting to local conditions.

'I am so well looked after, Emma. This week I'm doing the Drivers Education Program. The DoD wouldn't want anybody driving on the wrong side of the road or screwing up on a roundabout. That kind of thing isn't very good for Anglo-American relations!' he explained.

Tyler said that Bradley had been 'assigned' to look after him and help him settle in. That was why he was not exactly his pal. They didn't have all that much in common. It was a good idea, though—to have someone to show you the ropes, and help you get things sorted out—things like getting a car, for example.

'So what sort of car did you get?' Emma asked.

'I don't have one yet,' he admitted.

'Oh, but, how did you get here today?' she said.

'On the bus.'

'All the way from Exeter? It must have taken ages.'

'It's a long way, yes, but the scenery's pretty. Very English —kinda quaint.' Tyler blushed. Emma was rather gratified to know that he thought she was worth coming a long way for.

Tyler smiled at her. 'When I start looking for a new car, you can help me choose.'

Emma liked that idea – and it meant he'd like to see her again – but she shrugged and her reply was guarded. 'I have no idea what you're looking for. What did you drive, back home in the States?'

'A tractor, mainly.'

Emma laughed. 'Top speed?'

'Five miles an hour, on a good day. My folks are farmers.' Tyler surprised her by touching her hand. 'Today's a good day.'

His fingers were warm. Emma started to relax.

'What kind of car do you want?'

'I might look for something unusual, this time,' he said, 'like an old jeep, maybe. Something cool.'

The little place at the end of the pier had a jukebox. Tyler steered her in there. He got change from the bar and chose a song.

'Come and dance.'

'No! Nobody else is dancing,' Emma looked around at the other patrons; there were just a few people today, drinking and looking out at the water. The summer season hadn't yet begun. It was only April.

'They won't care, it's not busy. Come on! I don't think you're the shy type, really.' He pulled her hand and she followed.

Tyler seemed to come alive when he was dancing. Any awkwardness that she had felt when they were talking just melted away. When they danced, it was a different conversation, a free and easy one. It made her laugh and it made her feel good. She was pretty sure that she knew where it was leading.

\* \* \*

*March 1944*

The soldiers were told they would be billeted to various places around the city, and travel on to a proper army camp the following day.

Joe and about forty other soldiers would be spending the night in a church hall. They were told to behave themselves and not to deface parish property. A group of well-meaning local ladies helped them make a temporary dormitory on the polished parquet floor.

A plump woman with freckles and red hair kept tidy in a hairnet gave each man an enamel mug full of cocoa. Joe set his down beside his pack to cool down. He stretched himself out on a mattress filled with straw, and tried to relax.

The woman with the freckles turned and spoke to him, since he was the soldier nearest the door. 'What time shall I knock you up, dearie?'

Joe blinked, and there was an outbreak of raucous laughter.

The woman looked completely astonished, unable to understand why the soldiers found her so amusing, and why they kept repeating the remark to anyone who'd missed it.

Joe smiled pleasantly. 'Ma'am, where I come from, if you knock someone up it means you got 'em pregnant.' He hadn't meant to offend, but the poor woman went scarlet with embarrassment. Her face went redder than her hair.

Joe got slowly to his feet and apologised for being so rude. 'Begging your pardon, lady. Please, don't worry, our sergeant won't let us lie in bed all day.' There were a few more suppressed laughs at that.

'I... I understand you'll be moving on tomorrow,' she said stiffly, trying to recover her dignity.

'Yes, ma'am, but I can't tell you where.'

She looked as if she didn't care, as long as it was a long way away from her. She turned to escape the laughing eyes of all the young men.

Joe figured they'd be sent to the south coast. If they were going to invade France any time soon, they'd need to leave from somewhere down south. The powers that be would want to build up a mighty army ready to cross the Channel. Joe didn't think too deeply about that, he just hoped he'd see a bit of the beautiful English countryside from the train.

# Something to Hide

Susan Rowland had never been all that happy with her looks. Her mother—or the person she had always thought of as her mother—had been a beauty. On top of the piano at her parent's home there was a picture of Evelyn: an elegant woman with a heart-shaped face and a rosy mouth, with her honey-coloured hair cut in the classic 'pageboy' style of the 1940s. The photo had been 'colorized' by a painter, as photographs sometimes were, but it was reasonably accurate. Evelyn's eyes had been rendered in sapphire blue—they matched her engagement ring—and her mouth was a provocative pillar-box red.

George had thought that Evelyn was such a prize. A 'trophy wife' people called her. She didn't lose her figure, either, because for years and years there were no kiddies. Not until dear little Susan turned Evelyn into a rather glamorous mum.

Compared with all that, Susan was a plain Jane. 'Nothing wrong with that,' her parents would say, 'you've got a lovely nature, and that's what really counts.' They always adored their daughter. Susan had been a skinny kid and she grew into an angular young woman—she had always wondered why she didn't get her mother's hourglass curves.

Susan used to look in the mirror and worry about her hair, which was straight and brown. Not glorious strands of shiny caramel like Evelyn. Not even sandy brown like her dad's. Just dull brown. Susan had tried dying it various shades over the years, but somehow it didn't look right, certainly it never looked a bit like Evelyn's. It was almost a relief when it went grey. These days, Susan usually wore it in a neat, layered do, finishing abruptly beside her ear lobes. Sensible, if not exactly chic.

She had grown into her face a bit too. As a young woman, nobody ever thought of Susan as pretty. Even Keith thought of her as handsome, not pretty. She used to make a special effort to smile for photos, because if the camera caught her without a smile, she could look quite forbidding. She didn't want people to think she was glum, because she wasn't. She sailed through life making the best of everything.

Nowadays, she quite liked her suntanned, weather-beaten face, with all the fine lines that appeared when she smiled. Her face told a story of life lived to the full—it was a face that liked to be outdoors, a face that knew how to enjoy a joke—a kindly, practical sort of face.

Susan began to try to deal with the calamitous news about her pedigree. She told herself to buck up and get used to it. Of course it was hard to reconcile herself to the news that she was adopted—she'd liked the idea of belonging to the Old Devon Family—but she didn't really have any choice. Her reaction was natural, and her parents were not.

'You know the thing that makes me really angry, Emma?' she said. Emma didn't know—the whole thing seemed to make her mother angry.

'When I was pregnant with you, I had awful morning sickness—as I've often told you—and when I talked to my mother about it she actually had the gall to say that hers was worse when she was expecting me!'

'Grandma Evelyn must have really wished you were her own baby, Mum. It's a bit sad when you think about it.'

'Evelyn must have been off her head to think she could hide it. People must have wondered. Friends and neighbours must have speculated. In fact, I keep thinking of odd things people said, over the years. I feel so stupid because I didn't guess.'

'Grandma wanted to take her secret to the grave. She very nearly succeeded!'

'Yes, and now she's dead and beyond reproach—when there are a million questions that I need to ask her!'

Instead, Susan joined an organisation that supports people through the process of searching for their birth parents. She was a practical woman and she started by getting accustomed to the jargon.

'The term 'birth mother' seems fine,' she told Emma, 'but *'birth father?'* That doesn't seem quite right to me. I don't suppose he was involved in the birth at all. His contribution may have been rather more… fleeting.'

Susan applied for her original birth certificate and it revealed various things. It gave the name of her 'real' mother, Vera Sutton, but there was a blank space where the father's name should be. The address of the house where Susan was born was given, though, and it turned out to be the local Mother and Baby Home.

'Illegitimate. Awful word, isn't it?' Susan said, with a bit of a sigh. With her short grey hair and her crisp linen blouse, she was such a *respectable* sort of woman. If you didn't know she'd been a nursing sister you'd have picked an occupation with the same kind of aura—a headmistress or something.

'That's why no one uses that word any more. You do make an unlikely *love child*, mum, I have to say.' Emma patted her mother's arm. 'I'll do everything I can to help you find out more.'

'I know you will, dear. You've been a tower of strength.'

According to the pathetic little bits of information on the birth certificate, Vera must have been nineteen when she had Susan, and she came from London, although the Mother and Baby Home where she had Susan was quite close by—number 19 Seaview Road—only a short drive from the Rowlands' cottage. Emma and her mother went round there to see if the house was still standing. It was, but it had been converted into flats. Expensive flats.

'Maybe Vera came here to avoid the bombing,' Emma speculated, 'perhaps they thought it was safer than in London.'

'Funny. I don't remember anything,' Susan said, staring at the building as if the truth ought to be written across the front above the bay window.

'Of course not, Mum. Don't be daft. You need someone to tell you what happened.'

Emma got her camera out and took a photograph. It seemed like a fragile link with the past, this snapshot of Susan standing outside the building where she was born. Compared with the formidable history of the Old Devon Family stretching back in orderly generations to 1332, it seemed like something and nothing, but it was not. It was the first piece in the puzzle. The first glimpse of the real story.

* * *

In Emma's family it was always called 'seeing a film', although she had heard the expression 'going to the flicks'. Tyler called it 'catchin' a movie' —as if it was a communicable disease.

At the air base, Bradley was helping him to get ready for his big night. He found Tyler a tin of hair gel and showed him how to make the strands of hair at the front stand up on end. Tyler looked at himself doubtfully in the mirror.

'I don't know,' he said, 'I look like I've just had an electric shock.'

Brad laughed and told him to keep putting it on. 'The ladies like it. Which restaurant are you taking her to?'

'I'm not. We're going to a movie.'

'Take her to a restaurant, dumbo. You've got to buy her dinner if you're hoping to get into her—'

'Brad!'

'What are you going out with her for, if you don't want that?'

Tyler blushed. 'I like her. I want to get to know her—'

'I'll bet you do. That's why I'm trying to help. Take her to that little Italian place in town, with the soft music and the mood lighting. *Amore*, I think it's called. Buy her a nice dinner, make sure she has plenty of red wine. Keep refilling her glass for her, you hear? Then back to her place and don't you let her turn that light on when you get your foot inside the door. Then you hold her tight and pretend to trip over something. They always have stuff on the floor these single girls. Outfits they decided not to wear. Anyway, you fall over and you end up on the bed with her, and hey presto!'

Tyler stood still, with Bradley's tin of hair gel in one hand. He stared past his own reflection in the mirror, and looked, in horror, at Bradley's face instead. 'You don't think she'd expect all that, do you, on a second date?'

'She might. Depends on what type of girl she is. Personally I don't do a lot of second dates. Well, not if I get what I want on the first.'

'Brad. I don't think I need any more hair gel, thanks.' Tyler said. *Or any more advice*, he thought, and he frowned. He handed back the tin, and Bradley took it.

'Suit yourself.'

\* \* \*

Susan Rowland had her doubts about her daughter getting involved with someone new. 'What worries me, Emma, is that if you go and get fond of this fellow, what happens when he gets sent back to the States, or off to Germany or—or somewhere else?' Susan hardly dared mention the Middle East.

'There's nothing in it, Mum. It's just nice to be going out on a Friday night instead of sitting at home with you and Dad and the News at Ten.'

The doorbell rang and it was Helen, she had come over to help Emma get ready, since it was a 'proper' date this time. She came in carrying a dress bag on a coat hanger, and she hauled Emma upstairs to consider all the options for hair and makeup.

Susan went to the foot of the stairs. 'If there's nothing in it, Emma, then why do you need two hours to get ready?' she called out after them, but nobody was listening.

When Emma tried on Helen's dress she wasn't sure it was *appropriate,* to borrow Tyler's word for it. It was a strapless white dress with a bit of a frill instead of a skirt. Emma had a full-length mirror on the back of her wardrobe door, and she stood there, worrying. She tugged nervously at the hemline, trying to cover a bit more of her thighs. It slipped and revealed more cleavage. Then she hitched the top up and the skirt seemed shorter than ever. 'The top doesn't fit all that snugly, Helen. Not like it does on you. What if something, um… falls out?'

'He'll thank his lucky stars.'

'I'll wear a jacket. Or a cardigan.'

'No! Don't wear a jacket, and definitely not a cardigan—that would ruin the look completely. Leave your shoulder's bare, Emma, and show a bit of leg.'

'But, this is a dress for a nightclub, don't you think? Maybe I should go for something more casual?'

'It's great. I don't know why you are worrying anyway; he's already seen you in your swimsuit. You're just nervous,' Helen told her.

'I certainly am. After Matthew—'

'So that's what this is about. Stupid, hurtful Matthew. Don't you remember what they used to say at the Pony Club, when we were kids? The best way to get over a fall is to get straight back up there again,' Helen insisted, 'so keep your chin up. Think about how much you'd like Tyler to give you a ride!'

'Helen, for heaven's sake!' Emma didn't normally blush, but right now her face felt hot.

'That's put a bit of colour in your cheeks! Now, lipstick, let me see…'

\* \* \*

Adjusting to life in the military had been easy for Tyler. Growing up on his parents' farm had been just like being in the army. Long lists of chores to be done before sundown, and even longer lists of rules and expectations. To say that his parents were strict would be quite an understatement. The Robinsons were the type of people who didn't tolerate any kind of 'disrespect'. They wanted Sunday school behaviour all week. Tyler's room had to be kept neat and tidy at all times. No posters, no dirty socks, and definitely no smutty reading matter. At ten o'clock sharp it was lights out—provided he had folded his clothes, shined his shoes and washed behind his ears. Tyler could remember lying in his narrow bed at night, thinking about freedom and dreaming about love.

All the same, his parents were his parents and he didn't want them to worry. So just before he left the base, he rang his folks. They were very pleased he was settling in and making friends.

'Have you managed to connect with, you know, likeminded people?' his mother wanted to know.

Tyler had to confess he hadn't really worried about all that stuff since he arrived in Britain. He knew that she'd like to hear a catalogue of youth groups, guitar groups and other worthy activities.

'Well, what kind of socialising have you been doing?' His mother's voice rose sharply as she went into cross-questioning mode.

'I attended a dance the weekend before last. With my friend Bradley.' Tyler braced himself for the inquisition.

'Well I hope it was a decent sort of affair. Your father and I are a little concerned that—'

'Don't fret Mom, I'm having a great time. I met a young lady. I'm taking her out tonight.'

'Oh, Tyler, really? You may not be in England all that long. Wouldn't it be best to stick to wholesome activities with groups of people? Nothing too intimate. Nothing that might lead you astray. This girl—is she a respectable sort of person?'

'Of course. She's the sort of girl you'd really like.' Tyler said. Lying to his mother was easy now that the Atlantic Ocean lay between her and the truth.

'And you are going to be alone with her, tonight?'

'Yes.'

'Tyler, I shall worry about you. Will you promise me that you are not going to forget yourself?'

'I've got to go, Mom, my friend's giving me a lift into town.'

He took a moment to wash out the hair gel, though.

\* \* \*

The plan was to meet up on the pier. Emma was standing beside the doorway of the amusement arcade, and her dress had already excited a bit of comment from the young lads who frequented that establishment. Every wolf whistle made her feel worse. It was a little windy tonight and she was shivering. She really should have insisted on the cardigan.

Tyler came round the corner and almost walked straight into her.

'Oh. Emma. Oh my!' He was staring at the dress. He took a step backwards, and then another. Emma found herself wondering if he was about to turn and break into a run. She sighed.

'You don't like the dress, do you?'

'I, um, I… there's not that much to it, is there?' he blurted out. 'Aren't you cold?'

'Yes, I am. I am extremely cold. It's Helen's dress and I feel ridiculous in it. Do I look like a tart?'

Then a look of understanding came over his face and he softened. He took off his jacket—a beige zip-up thing that Emma's dad would have felt at home in, hardly a young man's jacket at all.

'Here,' he said, 'have this.' He put it around her shoulders.

Gratefully, she slipped her arms into the jacket—it was warm from his body. Deliciously warm. 'Thank you so much.'

'It's okay,' he said, and he gave her a sudden smile. 'I always wanted to do that.'

'Oh. Did you? I always wanted someone to do it for me.'

After that, it seemed a lot easier.

The cinema was tiny and the red velour seats were worn with age. Tyler liked it and he asked if it was 'an historic building'. The only thing Emma knew about its history was that it had been there since before the war, and that the building next door had been bombed, so it had narrowly escaped the same fate. She knew there had been a big crack in the wall on that side.

'It's not going to fall down on us, is it?' Tyler's eyes went wide, and then he knit his eyebrows and looked up and pretended he was gripped with fear, which would have been quite convincing except for the dimples.

'I hope not!' she laughed. Tyler took the opportunity to put his arm around her. 'You stick with me,' he said. 'I'll take care of you.'

The lights flickered out and they sat back to watch the film. It was a cowboy movie—Emma's choice—it seemed appropriate.

'You like cowboys, do you?' Tyler asked, whispering in her ear.

'I like horses,' she said crisply, not wishing to give him *too* much encouragement. She tried to smooth her short skirt down over her legs in a belated attempt at modesty. Good thing it was dark.

Afterwards they walked slowly back to Emma's car and he held her hand. They meandered along the road, wanting to spin it out. She asked him what he did for the Air Force, and hoped he'd kiss her soon.

'A lot of sheet-metal work, and oil changes, and brake jobs. But I'm interested in avionics,' he told her, 'that's all the computers and the instrumentation and stuff.'

'Isn't that a different, um, specialty?' she didn't like using that word, because it evoked a memory of Tyler's offensive friend, Bradley, but she used it anyway.

'Yeah. If I wanted to get involved in avionics I'd have to do more study, and I never was that great in school. I used to get a lot of C grades, you know,' he gave her an apologetic grin as he made this admission. Emma was used to this kind of remark— she was a teacher, after all. She gave him her best 'come hither' smile.

'But I do love fixing things,' Tyler said, failing to take the hint. 'Anything to do with engines and getting in there and taking stuff apart—and then putting it all back together again. I'll never stop liking that.' He sounded so keen and enthusiastic that Emma thought it would be easy to fall for him, if she didn't watch out. She wondered if he'd respond to telepathy, and tried it out: *Kiss me, Tyler, kiss me.* It was nice to have something, or someone, to take her mind off Matthew.

Emma knew what she was doing—comparing and contrasting—taking stock and trying to decide if Tyler measured up to her last boyfriend. She felt a little guilty, but she couldn't help it. Tyler was slightly taller than Matthew, which was a plus, because she liked to wear high heels. He was a little quieter than Matthew, which might be a minus. Matthew had been a confident, sweep-you-off-your-feet kind of guy. But then she remembered how Matthew used to like to air his opinions all the time, and she decided that she preferred Tyler. She'd like to know how Tyler's kiss would compare, that's for sure. She missed all that. She looked back at him and blushed. She hoped he wasn't reading her mind just now.

Tyler's eyes were a warm hazel colour, and he looked away sometimes when he spoke, as if he was a little unsure about what he was saying. Very different from Matthew's confident blue gaze.

Tyler admitted that after the dance, when he was trying to think of a way to bump into her again, he thought he'd had a brainwave when he remembered what she said about the swim club.

'I got this idea into my head that I could join up and then I'd get to see you every week,' he said. 'You can imagine my embarrassment when I realised that I wouldn't exactly blend in!'

Emma laughed. 'Not when every other member of the club is only so high and wears pink plastic strawberries in her hair.'

'Now I really liked the strawberries. I could get me some of those!

'Tyler, you idiot!' Emma laughed as they walked down the street. It was nice the way he didn't mind laughing at himself. Matthew would never have done that.

'Well, it meant I had to bite the bullet and ask you out, didn't it? Turns out it was all for the best.'

Then there was a lull in the conversation, so Emma told him what she knew about her mother's real origins, just for want of something else to say.

'I'm glad George and Evelyn let mum keep the name Susan, the name her birth mother gave her—Mum hated the idea that she'd been going around for sixty-five years not even knowing her own name.'

'That's something, I suppose.'

'She wants to know more, though, and so do I. I'd like to know what happened.'

'Well, gee Emma, we know what happened. He was a man, she was a woman, they did it and your mom turned up,' he said, letting the words tumble out fast in his haste to skim over the embarrassing bit.

'You make it sound so effortless! There's got to be more to it than that.'

'I always thought there was,' he said. 'The Devon story didn't seem to fit, somehow.'

For a poor student, Tyler's arithmetic was good—in a flash he worked out how old 'the unfortunate girl from London' would be now. A person who had been nineteen in 1945 would have been born in 1926. She would be well into her eighties. That cast doubt on the possibility that she was still alive.

'People do live to be that old,' Emma said, hoping against hope. 'Grandpa George is ninety-one, although he is a bit frail, now. I hope all this excitement isn't too much for him.'

Emma explained that in an effort to redeem himself with Susan, Grandpa George had been frantically trying to come up with information that would help to tell the real story of his adopted daughter's birth. Everyone knew everyone in this part of the world. He had divulged that one of the other residents at The Willows used to be a midwife at the Mother and Baby home where Susan was born.

'That's a great start,' Tyler said, 'Why don't we pay that little old lady a visit? Maybe she remembers Vera. At the very least she can tell us a bit more about the home for fallen women.'

'The what?'

'The place your mom was born.'

'Ok.'

'You know, Emma, this woman might be a dragon, if she used to work in a place like that—having a little one out of wedlock would have been frowned upon, I'm sure. A lot more than it is now. I feel sorry for poor Vera, having her baby in that kind of place. She would have been treated as a bad girl, most likely.'

'I suppose so, and she was only a teenager.'

'Yeah, she was. Shame on the guy, whoever he was. Anyway, we'll find out a little more next week.'

Emma was surprised that Tyler was prepared to do all this in his spare time but she knew he liked to keep finding reasons to see her and she wasn't going to say no. At the end of the night, she drove him to the bus depot in her car, and they said goodbye there.

He told her to hang on to the jacket. 'You don't need to wear your friend's clothes, you know. It's you that I like.'

She smiled at that. The bus was there and ready to go, all the other passengers were on board. Emma tried sending him one last little message, with that smile. She looked straight up into his eyes. *Last chance, Tyler, for a first kiss!* The bus depot was as good a place as any.

He hesitated, and looked as if he wanted to, but then he got out of her car and ran for the bus. There was such a look of re-gret on his face as he waved goodbye.

# First Base

The bones of the story began to emerge. The dragon from the home for fallen women turned out to be a cheerful woman with a recent perm and Zimmer frame. Her name was Mrs. Edgecombe. She was thrilled to have a visit.

Tyler knelt down beside her armchair to show her the certificate, and she put on her bifocals to have a look at the name. Tyler pointed it out for her. 'We were really hoping you might remember this girl, Mrs. Edgecombe. We kinda had this insane hope that you might know the whole story.'

Mrs Edgecombe shook her head. 'I don't, dear, I'm sorry to say. An awful lot of young girls came to the home during the last year of the war. We were kept very busy! It's the date that tells you the story. That baby would have been conceived in the summer of 1944.'

Tyler's expressive brows moved. He reckoned he knew what she was going to say. He gave a rueful smile, and glanced up at Mrs. Edgecombe. She wasn't afraid to be frank.

'Loads of girls from all over the place came here to help with the war effort. So many silly girls got their skirts lifted. The *story*—as you put it—was so often the same. *I met a soldier*. The South Coast was overflowing with soldiers, that year. This little town was teeming with them, and every other town nearby. The locals hadn't seen anything like it and never will again. Soldier boys everywhere you looked, and of course they all wanted to meet a girl and have a bit of fun before they met a bullet. Your lot were the worst,' she said to Tyler, as if he should apologise for them all, and accept responsibility for something that had happened long before he was born. He obliged her with a blush. She took off her specs and put them back in the case, still giving Tyler a reproachful eye. 'Girls didn't stand a chance with those flashy Yanks after them.'

Emma wasn't convinced. 'So you *think* that's what happened to Vera, but you don't remember her, and you don't know for sure.'

'I'll bet you a box of chocolates that's what happened, lovey,' Mrs Edgecombe said.

'But it could have been anybody. Not necessarily a soldier at all!'

'I have a feeling Mrs Edgecombe could be right.' Tyler said, but he didn't say why, and Emma found this rather unsettling. He was such a methodical, got-to-have-the-facts kind of person. He said you had to be like that to be a good mechanic. He didn't seem the type to leap to conclusions.

Mrs Edgecombe continued to reminisce. 'Yanks, we had here. Further up in the next bay, they had the British boys, but we got your lot.' She patted Tyler's arm. 'Churchill knew we were afraid of an invasion, and he said we'd have to fight them on the beaches. Then, we *were* invaded, but not by the enemy. Just a lot of young fellows like you.' The old lady sighed, re-membering times gone by. 'They said they'd be back. Cheeky devils. They upped and left quite suddenly. At the Mother and Baby Home, we had to deal with all the consequences, and there were a lot of consequences.'

Tyler thanked Mrs Edgecombe at great length for everything she'd told them, which wasn't much, as far as Emma was con-cerned, just a bit of speculation. He said she'd been most helpful and very kind, and they'd look into it all. He promised, with a hand on his heart, that he'd remember what she said about the box of chocolates.

\* \* \*

This time Emma drove him all the way back to the air base in her little car.

She pulled up to drop him off at the barrier, and Tyler hopped out quick and said goodbye. Emma tried to hide her disappointment, but it must have been obvious, because the soldier on duty at the barrier had a big smirk all over his face.

He called out to Tyler. 'Don't she get a kiss then, Robinson? Your lady friend?'

The remark really irritated Tyler, and it prompted him into a rash reaction. 'You know,' he said, 'I forgot. It just slipped my mind!' He turned back and waved to Emma not to go.

The guy at the barrier grinned in amusement. 'I can do it for you, if you don't know how,' he quipped. 'She looks quite tasty.'

'You just stay in your little box, thank you very much.' Tyler ran back to the car, and got back in.

Emma smiled nervously at him, and her heart skipped a beat when he pulled her towards him. Then, in classic Tyler fashion, he hesitated. At the very last minute, he turned his head away.

'What am I doing? I'm sorry, Emma. That guy is a jerk. This has nothing to do with him. I'd rather wait for everything to be perfect. You see—'

'Now would be fine, really it would,' she said, hoping the desperation didn't show. Honestly, Tyler could be *so irritating*. How could she hate him for it though? He was looking at her with his puppy dog eyes again.

'So, you'd be ok about it, even with that stupid guy over there gawking at us?' Tyler asked, and he stroked back a strand of her hair. She nodded, but they could both see that the man at the barrier was watching. In fact, he was grinning at them, and as soon as he saw that he had their attention, he puckered up his lips in imitation of a big smoochy kiss.

In the car, Tyler cringed with embarrassment. 'Oh my! I don't think now is the moment, Emma.'

'Why not?'

'It's just not how I imagined our first…'

'Tyler, I don't care. Do you want to do this, or don't you?'

'Yeah. Of course I do!' He sounded almost defensive, but he continued to hesitate.

'You could have fooled me. Anyone would think you–'

Tyler silenced her.

Suddenly it didn't matter why they were kissing, or who was watching. All that mattered was that they *were* kissing. Emma revelled in it. He tasted really good, and he smelt wonderful. A masculine scent mingled with shower gel and that stuff you spray on shirts when you iron them. Emma had been dreaming of being in his arms and enjoying a moment like this. She let her hand touch the side of his face, her fingers on his close-shaven skin, tracing down towards his jaw, while she enjoyed his kiss. She thought how much she'd like to run her fingers through his short, cropped hair. And the rest.

They paused for breath, and she looked up at him. 'That was rather good,' she said, in astonishment.

'Don't sound so surprised!' Tyler laughed and said he'd be offended if he didn't know her better. Then he kissed her some more. Emma's heart flipped inside her. He was a great kisser.

They were abruptly interrupted by an angry hoot from a car right behind them. It must have drawn up while they were preoccupied.

'That is a very rude man,' Emma said, and looked over her shoulder at the driver of the offending vehicle. She was almost tempted to give him the finger. Tyler glanced up too, and his hazel eyes widened.

'That's my commanding officer! Murphy's Law, huh?' He put his hand on the door handle. 'I'll see you Tuesday after school, in the library. There's a lot we can do there, now.'

'In the library?' she said, without enthusiasm.

'You want to carry on, don't you?'

Oh yes, she wanted to carry on, but not in a library. What a place for a hot date! She could think of more congenial venues. 'Why don't we...'

More angry tooting caused Tyler to leap out of the car. He made a salute to the fellow in the car—by way of apology—and ran off in the direction of the airbase.

Emma sighed and did a u-turn. She turned on the radio to keep her company on the long drive home, but when she heard the smooth voice of the DJ saying that *you can't hurry love*, she flicked it off in annoyance.

# Reasons, Fears and Excuses

Keith Rowland decided he should go and visit his father-in-law, at The Willows. Susan used to go round there twice a week, sometimes three times, before she found out she was adopted. These days she said she couldn't face it. Grandpa George felt that he'd lost his wife and his daughter in the space of a single week. He hadn't ever thought that anything would come between him and his beloved Susan. She was always daddy's girl.

Keith called out to George so that he didn't startle him, and let himself in with Susan's key. The old man was sitting in front of the TV, with the remote in his hand.

'Hello, George! How are you feeling?' Keith put the old man's mail on the side table for him.

'Keith! Where's Susie? Is she with you? Is she in the car?'

'No, I'm sorry to say that she isn't,' Keith said, with his usual Devon stoicism. 'Give her time.'

George sighed. 'I don't know how much time I've got left. I didn't anticipate spending the twilight of my life alone and friendless, rejected by my own daughter. And she is my daughter, Keith, I can't think of her any other way.'

'Of course she's your daughter. She talks like you, she digs the garden like you, she likes all the same books that you like, and the same type of teabags. Even the way she solves the crossword is like you, George.'

George looked miserably at the little side table that stood by his chair. The newspaper lay folded up at the page with the crossword on it. Most of the clues were solved and filled in.

'I wanted to ask her about number eight down,' he said, and his voice wobbled. He looked dangerously close to tears.

'She didn't get that one either,' Keith laughed, 'now isn't that a coincidence!'

'Why is she doing this to me, Keith?'

'She's in a bit of a huff, that's all. You know what she's like. It all came as a bit of a shock after all these years. I'm assuming that Evelyn was the one who insisted on keeping it a secret?'

'It seemed like the best policy, Keith. You have to try to understand. People said you didn't know what you were going to get when you adopted a child. It might be from 'bad blood', whatever that meant. Evelyn didn't want anyone to think that about her little baby. She was so thrilled when we got Susie.'

'Yes, but George, Susie has been grown up for ever such a long time. Surely you and Evelyn could have let her know—when you thought she was old enough to understand?'

'I did wonder if we should. Especially more recently—times have changed and people are much more open about these things now. Last week I was sitting having a quiet cup of tea in that café on the promenade, and there were two women in there having a conversation about IVF and sperm samples! As bold as brass. Not a hint of embarrassment. Talking away like you and I might have a chat about the weather or the football. It was unbelievable.'

'I am of the opinion that it's better to be open about things, George. I do wish Evelyn—'

'Evelyn was a wonderful mother to Susan. She loved her like her own. Everyone thought it was for the best that Susan believed she *was* our own. There never was a time when we wanted to go back on that decision. I wish I'd burned those ruddy papers.'

'I think Susan is glad that you didn't. I believe the real story is very precious to her. You know Emma's going to try to find out what happened? She's met a young man who says he'll help her look into it all. They found out the name of Susan's real mother—'

'Evelyn was Susan's 'real' mother! The person who fed her and dressed her and fetched her from school all those years!'

'Apologies, George. Bad choice of words, you know what I'm like,' Keith said, deciding not to go on any further with the tale of Emma's discoveries. 'Let's talk about something else, shall we?'

'Yes. You can tell me all about this young man that Emma's been walking out with. I want to know if he's good enough for her. I hope he's not like that time-waster in Manchester. Does the boy have prospects, Keith? I don't suppose you've thought about that, have you? And what are his intentions, I wonder?'

Keith smiled, and sat down on the ottoman. 'I'll tell you all I know,' he said, 'but the first thing I can say is that young people don't take kindly to any enquiries about prospects and intentions, George. So when Emma brings Tyler round to see you, as I'm sure she will, you can't talk about any of that.'

'That's where parents are letting their kids down these days, in my opinion. You shouldn't stand by and let Emma get treated like a woman of easy virtue. You should put your foot down, Keith. With a firm hand.' George's own hand shook as he pointed an accusing finger at his son-in-law.

'Oh George, if you only knew how worried I am. He's not from round here, you see. He's from Idaho.'

'Best known for its potatoes,' George said. 'You need to find out a bit more about him than that! And quick sharp too, before Emma gets her heart broken. You know as well as I do that she rushes into things.'

'Susan says we mustn't interfere—we must let it run its course. Don't encourage it, and don't discourage it, that's what she says.'

Grandpa George snorted, 'sounds like some rubbish from a women's magazine to me. Beats me how those publications get away with it. They don't tell women what's good for them.'

'Emma can think for herself, George, and we have to remember that she is a grown up, no matter how much we want to protect her. Young women do get hurt, but what will be will be. He sounds like a nice enough boy.'

'That's exactly what you said last time.'

# 9

## The Library

Emma wasn't keen on heavy reading. On a warm afternoon in early May she would rather have done some courting in the sand dunes. That was the only kind of heavy she was interested in. She sighed. Tyler obviously wasn't the type to rush these things. He was sitting opposite her, studying a book, and on the table between them there was a large plastic sign saying that eating, drinking, talking, and smoking were all strictly prohibited. She had no doubt that kissing and cuddling would also be frowned upon, so she tried to put all that out of her mind, even though the secluded corner by the foreign language dictionaries looked quite inviting.

She couldn't disturb Tyler; he was completely immersed in a large tome about World War Two, all full of line drawings of Panzers and Sherman tanks and Spitfires. She turned back to the social history of war that she had found. She might as well have stayed late at school and made a start on her end-of-term reports.

Emma read that over a million American soldiers were stationed in the south of England at approximately the right time. They had time on their hands and money in their pockets. They practised their manoeuvres by day and they practised their manoeuvres by night. In the absence of their American sweethearts, they made do with the local girls. The book said that the guys didn't think much of the way British women dressed, but the solution to that was to take their clothes off, wasn't it? Emma learned that thousands and thousands of illegitimate babies were born the very same year as her mother. It was all rather shocking really.

'Mum was born in January, so she was probably conceived sometime in May,' Emma said. She had to speak low to avoid upsetting the librarian, and whispering seemed to emphasize the clandestine nature of the conversation.

Tyler looked up and frowned. 'In that case, maybe the guy didn't know he was going to be a father. Maybe that's why he didn't do the decent thing. It's possible he didn't find out that his girl was pregnant before he had to go.'

'Go where?'

'What?' Tyler looked surprised.

'Where did he have to go?' she said.

'Emma, baby, June the 6th—D-day? The Normandy Landings? It's the single most important event in military history. In world history, perhaps.'

'Ah.'

* * *

Despite her inadequate grasp of military history, and his disinterest in the foreign language dictionaries, Emma and Tyler got on all right that day. They made a good team. They pieced together bits of information from a whole pile of books, passing them from one to the other when they found something that might be relevant. They quizzed the librarian for other avenues to explore. They sussed out the name of a local historian who could tell them a little more.

Tyler rang him up and made an appointment to drive over and see him later that day, and the man seemed pleased to help. He promised to dig through his records and sort out some photos. Tyler said he looked forward to it, and he and his girl would see him soon. Emma could have hugged herself in anticipation. It wasn't the thought of the local historian, obviously. It was just so lovely that Tyler took it for granted that they would go together—that was the important thing. And he called her 'his girl'!

Tyler asked her if he could drive her car. 'I'm old fashioned,' he explained. 'I'm the guy and I like to do the drivin'—you don't mind, do you, Emma?' She didn't mind at all. When he pulled into a quiet country lane, she was even more delighted.

He nosed the car into a secluded place among the cowslips, and turned the engine off.

'We're a little early,' he said with a smile, 'but I think I know how we can kill some time.' He unclipped his seatbelt, and hers. Then he turned to her and put his arm around her. 'Don't worry,' he told her, 'I'd never take advantage, but I sure would like the chance to get to know you better.'

Emma was very, very receptive to that idea. The moment his mouth met hers she knew she was going to enjoy being Tyler's girl.

* * *

The local historian, Jack Bovey, made them a cup of tea, and showed them his impressive collection of war memorabilia. He had helmets and gas masks and ration books and all manner of stuff. He even had a table set out with a big map showing where the various groups of soldiers landed, and all the battles they fought as they made their way into France and Germany. Emma thought he sounded very keen and enthusiastic, like a boy scout or a sergeant major in the Home Guard. She tried to steer him back to the things no one remembers anymore. She asked him why he thought Vera had come to the South coast in the first place.

Jack told them what he knew about the women who were part of the war effort. 'A bevy of lovely ladies', he called them. 'There were Red Cross nurses, pretty little WAAFs and

WRENS, and don't forget the Land Girls, of course, digging for victory.'

Emma explained that the birth certificate said that Vera, her newly discovered grandmother, was a canteen worker with the NAAFI.

'Yes, yes. It stands for the Navy, Army and Air Force Institutes, set up in 1921. There was a NAAFI canteen in a Nissen hut opposite the railway station—right here in the middle of town. It was handy for the soldiers getting off the train. Lots of young women did a stint in the NAAFI. They provided various types of refreshment for the troops. 'Serving the Services' was their motto. Their brief was to meet the recreational needs of the armed forces.'

Tyler nearly choked on his tea.

'And to help the lads keep up their morale,' Jack said, taking no notice. 'They were indispensable during World War Two. NAAFI canteens were for British personnel, of course, but when Eisenhower started pouring his men into the area as part of Operation Bolero, the NAAFI girls pitched in and did what they could for the American boys too.'

Emma and Tyler exchanged a glance. It had to be said that this man Jack was thoroughly steeped in it all. He spoke as if the war was a well-organised game of hockey or an exciting treasure hunt, as some military enthusiasts do. It didn't tell them much about Vera, though.

'You'll be astonished when I show you this,' Jack said excitedly, like a kid with a new conker. Emma and Tyler prepared to be suitably astonished. Jack went over to his desk and brought back a stack of dusty old books, which turned out to be photograph albums, each one filled with small black and white photos. Each photo was carefully mounted using those fiddly little corners people used to use. Jack had book-marked a page in one of the albums. It was a fuzzy little picture of a trio of girls standing outside a big tent. He passed it to Emma, for her to look at. 'Read the caption, underneath.'

Emma looked at the names, written in pen and ink under the photograph. 'V. Sutton—V for Vera. That's my grandmother!'

'I knew you'd be pleased,' Jack said. 'I was, too, when I found that. I'm a mine of useless information, or a treasure trove, depending on how you look at it. Rarely do I get the chance to help someone like this, though. I couldn't believe my luck when I saw that name.'

Emma just stood staring at the image in front of her, wanting to know the woman, to understand her. 'She doesn't look a bit like mum,' she said, after a while, 'or me.' She seemed a little disappointed.

'No, she doesn't' Jack said, glancing over her shoulder, 'she's a real blonde bombshell, that one. Gorgeous thing!'

Emma didn't say anything. She knew that you just had to get used to people making that kind of remark. She'd heard the line about blondes having more fun, but she didn't like the subtext. She liked being a brunette.

Tyler touched Emma's arm. 'I'd say you must look more like your granddaddy. He'd have been tall, dark and handsome, I reckon.'

*Nice save, Tyler*, she thought. *That was a sweet thing to say.*

\* \* \*

On their way home to the base Emma invited Tyler to the cottage on Friday—for a family dinner with her parents. She wouldn't normally drag a guy home after so brief an acquaintance, but Tyler kept asking about her mum and dad, and he really seemed to be angling for an invite. He said how much he envied all the guys who lived off base—the ones who had the luxury of being in military family housing, although nobody except Tyler considered those mean little dwellings to be luxurious.

Tyler thought they must be bliss, though, compared with being in the dorm with the other single guys. Comfy lounge suites, your own TV, a little backyard for a barbeque. He knew that one of the guys even had a classic car in his garage; he took it apart every weekend. Emma laughed and said that was an odd way to unwind after a week spent maintaining aircraft.

'Those guys are so lucky,' Tyler said, 'goin' home every night to a nice dinner with their families, and some good conversation. I do miss that of an evening. You know, relaxing with folks you get along with.' His voice was plaintive and hopeful.

Eventually it seemed easier just to ask him home to dinner.

Emma wasn't sure how Tyler would get on with her parents. She was acutely aware that her parents were older than the average, as they'd chosen to have Emma rather late in life. They seemed to have very fixed opinions on things.

'You're so fortunate, Tyler. Your mum and dad belong to a younger generation, and their mindset will be closer to your own. They'd be a bit more open-minded, maybe?'

'Parents are parents wherever you go, Emma. And my folks, well, I wouldn't call them open-minded, exactly.'

More than that he would not say.

* * *

*April 1944*
Joe thought she looked just like a porcelain doll.

A long time ago in a second-hand shop in town, he'd seen one in the window. She was so pretty, he had to go in and ask if he could have a closer look. Maybe he could get her for his little sister. They said the doll was French, and had once been very expensive. Her face was made of porcelain, pale and delicate, with a hint of pink on her cheeks and an irresistible little pink mouth. She had blue eyes that closed when you tipped the doll up and laid her on her back, and curled dark lashes. He wished he could have got her for his sister, but she was still too expensive, even second or third hand.

This girl in the canteen had that look about her. She had fluffy blonde hair, which she had set into pin curls around her face. It had gotten a little dishevelled now, in the heat of the steaming cookhouse. China blue eyes; lashes darkened with mascara and curled, just like the antique doll.

She lowered those lashes when she saw him looking at her. He was going to look away, pretend he hadn't been staring, but he didn't. Why should he? He smiled, and she smiled right back. He knew her name too, he heard another guy say 'Hiya, Vera'.

There was a group of soldiers on the next table, and they had seen her too. Joe heard them plotting and planning. One of them nodded his head at the girls behind the counter.

'Did you try asking her, the little cockney sparrow?' one of the soldiers said. He pointed at Vera with his thumb. She was standing by an enormous tea urn talking to her co-worker—a tall pale young woman with her brown hair tied back with a ribbon.

'You mean the blonde, she told me to get lost,' the second one said.

'What about the other one, with the nice...' The soldier's hands delineated the nice part.

'No luck there, she's a *lady*,' said the third.

The first soldier leant forward in a conspiratorial fashion and spoke low to his three friends.

'Those two—they finish here about nine o'clock. They always walk home along Lighthouse Lane. They lodge in one of those cottages beyond, right on the headland.'

'What are you saying, Orville?'

'There are trees along that lane, and it's quite secluded. We could be there to meet 'em.'

'You mean to jump them?'

On the next table, Joe didn't like the sound of that. He stirred his cocoa and looked in the opposite direction, hoping the men wouldn't see that he was listening. It was hard to hear the words —he dare not look at their faces—but his concentration was intense.

'Why not? There are four of us, and two of them. It'd be easy.'

'I don't think so, Orville, you can get into big trouble doing something like that.'

'That one over there, the snooty one, she won't give me the time of day. She said she only talks to officers.' In an action that did not match his words, the soldier gave the girl a wave and touched a finger to his cap. She gave a tiny have-to-be-civil smile. 'The way I look at it they owe us, don't they? We're fighting their war for 'em.'

'It's our war now.'

'Look, guys, you do what you like, but I'm not having anything to do with it. I can get me a girl the usual way. I just talk 'em round, you know. No need to do anything stupid.'

'Oh, yeah? And when did you last get a girl, Tony? In Chicago?'

'Orville's right. They'll send us over soon, I know they will. We could all be dead.'

'That's no way to talk.'

'Who's in front, that's what I'm asking. My Dad always said you gotta look around and see who's in front, who's gonna take the flack. Here we are, right on the coast, looking out across the sea. There's nothing and no one between us and the enemy, is there? There isn't anyone in front to take the bullets. We are the front. We go over, we'll take the bullets. I'm not facing that without a little something to make me feel better.' He drained his cocoa as if it was a double whisky and they got up to leave. 'I say we jump those girls. Tonight.'

Joe looked at the girl with the china doll face. She was refilling the urn with water. He wondered what her pretty face would look like in the morning.

# 10

## Family Dinner

'This place must get photographed for calendars and stuff all the time!' Tyler said, when he saw the Rowlands' cottage.

'Well, not exactly. I think we have had the occasional Japanese tourist take a photo outside,' Emma said, trying to lead him up the garden path, in the literal sense.

'I'm not surprised. I wish I had a camera, now. My mom would love to see a picture of a cute little house like this.' He kept looking up at the thatched roof and the window boxes and everything.

'Come on, come on. They'll wonder what we're doing out here, Tyler.'

'Of course, best behaviour, I promise.'

'Oh, speaking of which—can I ask you a HUGE favour?' Emma paused, with her hand on the door.

'Anything,' he said, and he dimpled at her in a very winsome way.

'Can we not talk about Iraq?'

'Ok,' he said obediently, 'I wouldn't want to offend them.'

'And I wouldn't want *them* to offend *you*,' she said, as she opened the heavy wooden door. Tyler followed her in, and padded along behind her like a big Labrador.

He was marvellous with them and she needn't have worried. With his old-fashioned manners and his farm boy charm, Tyler was instantly in tune with them. Keith Rowland, who was a little deaf, had a bit of trouble understanding Tyler's soft American drawl, but before long they were all getting on famously.

Naturally, Emma's father wanted to know all the details about Tyler's role in the United States Air Force, for a start. 'So you don't actually fly at all, then?' Keith said, with just a hint of the disappointment Tyler was accustomed to.

'No, for every single person who gets to fly there are about a hundred on the ground, you know.' Tyler was patient and polite.

'Really? As many as that?'

Tyler told them a wonderful anecdote about the time when Lord and Lady Something-or-other came to inspect the base, and see some of the aircraft.

'Her Ladyship was all dressed up nice, and she was wearing this enormous pink hat, you know—the type with the wide brim —like Princess Diana used to wear. Anyway, she was standing waiting to address the guys, and there was a misunderstanding and someone started cycling up the engine on one of the planes. You probably know this, Mr Rowland, but jet engines suck up a huge volume of air when they're running—and the hat just took off and went straight through the engine. It was *dust* in seconds, basically. If you'd have blinked you would have missed it. Some of the other guys were like 'where'd the hat go?' I mean, it wasn't funny, but in a way it was. Her Ladyship was absolutely amazing, I have to say. She just handled the incident with such *aplomb.* That has to be the only word for it. Aplomb. She acted as if NOTHING had happened. She gave her speech, shook everybody's hand, as if her hat getting shredded was all part of the plan. She was, like, so dignified. So we all said 'Hats off to her', as you can imagine.'

'Oh, you didn't!' Susan Rowland said, with a smile.

'No, we didn't. Not to her—she was too nice. We said it a lot afterwards though. We've been saying it ever since.' He laughed and flashed his eyes at Emma.

Emma could see that with that story, they were won. It wasn't the story, of course, it was the charming way he told it, smiling and laughing and looking so young and happy. He squeezed Emma's hand. 'There's just something about you British girls, isn't there? You are just so refined.' His warm hazel eyes twinkled at her as he spoke.

Susan and Keith looked at one another and started asking Tyler a number of searching questions about how long he was going to be in the UK, and the stability of his position with the air force. Was he ever likely to see active service? Or get posted anywhere dangerous? That kind of thing. Emma could have died of embarrassment. One thing that emerged from the grilling was that Tyler was more than two years younger than her. This was something of a revelation to Emma, as it had not come up in any of their conversations so far. He was only twenty-two, and she was already twenty-four.

Mrs Rowland decided it was time to serve the roast beef.

* * *

After dinner, Tyler went and got his laptop out of Emma's car. He had brought it with the intention of helping Emma and her mum do some research on the internet, which might help uncover the truth about Vera.

Emma was glad to introduce a diversion. So far the conversation had gone well, but she wasn't sure how long her parents would hold up under cross-questioning. Emma had gone on and on at them beforehand about things they could say and things they couldn't. Susan and Keith had been made to promise not to share any of their thoughts on the Bush Administration. They too had been instructed not to mention Iraq. Or Vietnam. Or Cuba. She was especially keen for them to keep quiet about their participation in the Campaign for Nuclear Disarmament.

'Try to find common ground,' Emma had begged.

Susan had promised she would try, but the only thing that sprang to mind was that she too had once been closely associated with an Air Base. She had spent a whole summer in a tent outside RAF Greenham Common, as part of the women's peace camp. Of course, that was a long time ago, when Emma was no more than a twinkle in Keith's eye, and she wasn't about to embarrass her daughter with all of that!

'Shall I plug this in and get it up and running for you, then?' Tyler said, much to Susan's relief, and without further ado they scurried round trying to find a suitable power point for the laptop. They trawled though the marriage records to try to find out if Miss Sutton ever met Mr Right.

Tyler and Emma worked for several hours before they struck gold. After they found her married name the rest was easy.

'All we need to do is find out where she is now,' Tyler said.

'She'll be dead and buried, that's where she'll be,' Keith said. Vera would be well into her eighties. He didn't want Susan getting her hopes up.

The British Telecom records showed that Vera Sutton, who was now Vera Fitchett, still occupied an address in East London. There was even a phone number.

Susan sat on the chintzy couch and tried to come to terms with the idea of contacting Vera. If she chose to, she could ring up a total stranger and say 'Hello, you're my mum, why didn't you keep me?' It seemed like total insanity.

Susan said that when she joined the support group for adopted people they had asked her to abide by their 'code of ethics' —they did not advise surprise phone calls and dropping in on people like a bolt out of the blue. Confronting them about what may have been one of the most embarrassing or unhappy episodes in their whole life should be done with tact and discretion. They recommended going through an intermediary to make sure that the 'other party' welcomed the contact from the long lost child. She knew that in many cases the birth mother refused to meet, and said it was all too painful. If that turned out to be the case then Susan wouldn't want to upset her. After all, Vera would be a frail old lady.

'Mum, how will you ever find out anything about your father if you are afraid to ask her?'

'Don't push me, Emma. I can see that you are impatient to know everything, but really, I must stick to the code of honour put forward by my Support Network. I have signed to say that I will abide by that code. If Vera doesn't want contact we have to respect that.'

She changed the subject—she asked Tyler about life on the base.

'I hear it's like stepping onto American soil, going in there.' she said.

'Technically, it is. We are very well provided for. We got the United States mail, for sending letters home, and we can even use the dollar as currency. They have all the shops that we are used to, so I bought my Levis over here. It's not like home though, really. Not like being with your folks. Seeing the people you care about every day. I miss that a lot.'

'Of course you do,' Susan felt a wave of maternal feeling for the poor boy—he sounded almost woebegone.

'Not that I have anything to complain about,' Tyler added, with puppy dog eyes, 'except for feeling a little homesick. They take real good care of us. Everything is so well organised. There are a lot of rules and regulations—but that's just to make everything go smoothly, of course. Still. I sometimes wish I lived off base, in a place of my own, or at least in military family housing.'

'Then you could do as you pleased, in your time off?' Keith asked.

'Well, maybe a bit more than I do living in the men's dorm. But even in military housing there are lots of rules and regulations... just last week a memo went round saying that waterbeds are expressly forbidden in homes owned by the Department of Defence.'

'Why come down so hard on the waterbeds? —If you get my drift,' Keith suppressed a bit of a laugh, 'do they represent a security risk? Not watertight, perhaps? Is it just the Air Force that can't have them? Perhaps if Tyler was in the Navy a waterbed would be just the ticket!'

'Dad! What did I tell you about being facetious!' Emma said, and punched her father playfully on the arm.

'It sounds kinda dumb, but they had their reasons. Apparently there was a little house where the family went to a lot of trouble getting the bed up the tiny stairs—you know how small some of these British places are, and then the floor wasn't strong enough and it fell through and created one hell of a mess,' Tyler explained. 'So after that, no more waterbeds.'

'Awful things, waterbeds,' Susan remarked, 'probably quite sensible to ban them really. We encountered one when we went away for our anniversary, didn't we, Keith? I was just lying there in my negligee, and Keith was, um, quite keen to join me, I suppose, and he jumped on the bed and I was sort of *tossed aloft* on a great wave. Really! I was almost thrown out of the bed. Intimacy was virtually out of the question! There must be a special knack to it.'

Keith and Susan laughed together as they shared this warm memory of their holiday, but the young people looked a little uncomfortable.

Tyler thought he'd better say something. 'I wouldn't really know. I always slept in a regular bed, back home in Idaho.'

Susan smiled at Keith, and asked him to help her wash up the coffee cups. She wanted to give the youngsters some time alone.

As soon as Emma knew that her mother was out of earshot she told Tyler what she wanted to do.

'Vera's eighty-four now, and she won't last forever. I want to know the story, and she's the only one who can tell us. I don't want to wait a hundred years for an intermediary to try and fail to get an audience with her. I want to ask her, straight out.'

'What about the code of ethics? Your mum said she signed to say she would abide by it.'

'Yes, Tyler. She signed—but I didn't sign anything, did I?'

He paused, looking at her face, and then he smiled. 'So you're thinking…'

'That's what I'm thinking. I'm going to go up to London and try to meet her,' Emma said.

Tyler only had to think for a second, and then he made a decision. 'I could come with you,' he said. 'If you'd like that.'

Pleased as she was that Tyler wanted to do this, Emma was doubtful about letting him get involved.

'I'm not sure,' she said, 'I mean I'd really like you to come, but—you don't think she might find it intimidating, do you?'

Tyler gave her a devastating grin. 'Me? I won't intimidate her. I'll be real nice to her. It might even help.'

'How?'

He smiled his dimpled smile at her. 'Emma—the one thing we already know about her is that she likes American boys.'

* * *

*April 1944*

Vera and her co-worker, whose name was Miranda, hung up their aprons at ten past nine. They put on their coats and set off for 'home', which was, for the time being, an attic room in a draughty cottage on the headland. They had been working together in the canteen for less than a month, but it seemed like forever in terms of experience. Time seemed to be measured in a different way in wartime. Miranda felt she'd lived more in the last few weeks than in the last twenty years—her whole lifetime.

The women walked along the road companionably, even though Vera was a barrowman's daughter from the East End of London, and Miranda's people were rather upper crust. The blackout was diligently enforced—nobody wanted to attract the unwelcome attentions of the Luftwaffe—and the street was very black indeed. It was hard to see the way unless there was moonlight, and tonight there was none.

Nearer to the centre of the town the houses were terraced—not in neat regular terraces like London townhouses—just little houses leaning drunkenly against one another. The whole town was a curious hotchpotch of styles that the American boys found very quaint and amusing. Further along the route the cottages were more spaced out, individual little places with hedges and gardens around them. At the end of the lane, just before the path that led up to the headland, there was a dark coppice of trees.

Each night for the last three weeks, Miranda had felt afraid, walking past those trees—but tonight seemed easier somehow. She and Vera had formed a closer alliance of late. They worked together, they slept in the same little room and in their free time they went everywhere together—to the shops to see if there was anything to buy, or to the cinema to see the newsreels.

Their landlady only allowed one bath per week, and a shallow one at that. Miranda had hers on Saturday, like most people did. She wanted to be presentable for church. Vera negotiated hard and got permission for a Wednesday night dip. The girls operated a system of using up the other one's bathwater—they took turns as to who went in first—it was a way of getting an extra hot bath.

Tomorrow afternoon was their day off. They were going to a tea dance at the King's Hotel, and Vera was going to cut Miranda's hair and show her how to set it in Hollywood curls. Miranda wasn't sure that her parents would approve, but she was driven by her quest to attract a young officer. An RAF pilot, maybe. The NAAFI canteen was for the junior ranks, so Miranda needed to cast her net a little wider.

'Your ma and pa are tucked up in their vicarage in Hemel Hempstead. What the eye don't see the heart don't grieve after,' Vera told her, 'you wait—I can make you look like a million dollars. You'll have to beat them off with a stick!' They both laughed and tried not to miss their footing in the dark.

That was the moment when the men jumped the girls.

# 11

## Meeting Vera

Together they talked about the trip to London. Tyler really wanted the chance to do some sight seeing. He had such a long list of places he wanted to see that Emma said they'd need days, and he laughed and said that would be fine with him. He wanted to see the Houses of Parliament, and Bucking-HAM Palace, obviously. He'd heard you couldn't actually drive past Number Ten, but he wouldn't mind seeing the Tower of London and Madame Tussauds. Oh, and the millennium wheel thing. Emma smiled. Exploring London for days on end with Tyler. It seemed a rather nice idea. Almost dreamy, in fact.

Then Tyler said he needed Emma to give him some advice. His mom's birthday was coming up and he wasn't sure what she'd like. He was going to organise the usual bunch of flowers by Interflora, but he wanted to do something more.

'She says she really misses seeing me around the place,' he said, and he reached into his backpack to get something out. 'So I thought about sending her this.' He'd had a photograph of himself enlarged and put in a frame. In the photo, he was standing right beside the nose of a fighter plane, and he was wearing camouflage combat pants and a black t-shirt. He looked every inch the handsome soldier boy. Every single inch, from the roots of his dark hair, cropped close to his head, to the toes of his heavy, masculine boots.

'It was taken when I first arrived in Britain. What do you think, Emma?'

Emma stared at the photograph, transfixed. 'I think anyone would like to get him for their birthday!'

'She is my mother, Emma,' he said. 'Maybe it's too—'

'No, it's great, Tyler. She'll be so proud to show that to all her friends and neighbours, don't you think?'

'Yeah. She has a lot of friends who stop by all the time. Sewing bee people and all that.'

'Well. They'd all like a look at her very attractive son, wouldn't they?' Emma said, and watched him colour up a little. He was quite flattered all the same.

'I'll pack it up and mail it to her, then.'

'Good idea—and Tyler?'

'Yep?'

'Do you think I could have one, for *my* birthday?' She smiled at him and caught his eye.

'What do you want one of those for, baby, when you got the real thing?' he said, and laughed as he pulled her into a kiss.

Emma couldn't wait to be alone with him in London.

* * *

They sped along the motorway in Emma's little car, with him at the wheel, of course.

'You seem to have got the hang of driving on the left, then, thank goodness,' Emma said to him as they drove along.

'Yeah, it's no problem now. I did the Drivers Education Program at the base. Roundabouts were real hard at first, but I've got it figured out now.'

She smiled at him. He looked great today, in his short-sleeved navy shirt. His dark hair had grown a little longer since they first met, and you could see that it had a bit of a wave in it. He touched the side of his face, self-consciously.

'Did I miss a bit when I was shavin' or something?'

'No. I was just enjoying the view,' Emma said, with a grin. He looked quite pleased, but he blushed and pretended to concentrate hard on the driving.

'Speaking of seeing the sights, Tyler, shall we see if we can get on the boat trip on the Thames this morning? Then we could call on Vera in the afternoon.'

'Yeah, that's a plan,' he said, 'the afternoon's probably more appropriate, isn't it?

'I don't know if there is an 'appropriate' time to ask someone how they got into trouble. Etiquette has to take a back seat, maybe.'

Tyler smiled, and made an unusually forthright remark. 'Perhaps that is how she got into trouble. On the back seat!'

Emma smiled to herself. They didn't need the back seat. They were booked into a hotel tonight.

* * *

Mrs Fitchett, who was once Miss Sutton, the blonde bombshell, now lived in a small terraced house in East London.

Emma's car was parked, strategically, a few houses down the street. They'd knocked at the door and there was no one in, but the next-door neighbour had told them that 'Missis F' had only popped up to the shops to get her pension. This gave them a chance to observe the animal from a safe distance before they went in for an actual encounter. Mrs Fitchett was a very long time. They began to think she'd rumbled them and had gone in round the back.

When the moment finally came, Emma and Tyler sat in the car, taking turns with the binoculars.

'That could be her!' Emma said, 'one elderly lady with a headscarf and a basket. You want a look?' She passed him the binoculars.

'I'd say she's been shopping,' Tyler said, 'she's bought herself a nice lamb chop for dinner, or maybe it's sausages. You English love your bangers and mash, don't you?'

Emma punched him lightly on the arm. 'Maybe that is her. There is something about her that reminds me of mum, you know.'

'Yeah. There's just something, isn't there?'

'Wait and see if she goes into number 20.'

They watched with bated breath as the woman walked slowly up past number 18.

'She's slowing down,' Emma said.

'Maybe she is,' Tyler watched closely, trying to interpret the signs.

They were both most gratified when the woman opened the gate of number 20, went in, and closed it behind her with care. They smiled at each other as she got out her key to open the front door. They watched her go inside.

'That's Vera.'

Eventually they had to get up the courage to go and knock on her front door.

\* \* \*

'Hello. Mrs Fitchett?' Emma began,

'I've got a pan of milk on the boil,' Mrs Fitchett said, in a suspicious edgy tone. She had a chain on her door, and she didn't take it off. She spoke to them through a small gap. Emma was afraid the old lady thought they were Jehovah's Witnesses or something.

'I'm sorry to bother you but—just let me explain why I would like to talk to you. You see I'm from Devon, and my family lives near Torbay, and we recently found some old papers that led us to you, because—'

'Oh my gawd, you're Susan!'

'No. No. I'm not Susan. I'm Emma, Susan's daughter. Susan is in her sixties now, Mrs Fitchett.'

'Her sixties? Susan?' She said. She seemed quite stunned and flustered. '*In her sixties?* They don't stay young for long, do they?'

Tyler introduced himself with his usual elaborate politeness. Vera cocked her head on one side like a curious budgerigar when he spoke.

'You're one of them, aren't you?'

'Ma'am, I do hail from the United States, if that's what you mean, and I would sure appreciate it if you could just talk to us for maybe two minutes. Just two minutes of your time, Mrs Fitchett, could you spare us that? We've come a long way to see you.' He smiled his devastating smile at her and moved his eyebrows like an irresistible puppy dog.

The door closed for a moment, but only so that Vera could take the chain off. She ushered them into her parlour, which had a big brown couch with those lacy doily things that old people use to protect the arms of their furniture from getting grubby.

'Do you need to turn off that pan of milk, Mrs Fitchett?' Tyler looked across at her and raised his eyebrows in genuine concern. He didn't want to be the cause of a mishap.

'Oh, you are an innocent flower, aren't you?' Vera said. Emma had to whisper to him that there was no milk.

'I've got to take care of myself, haven't I?' Vera said, with a smile. 'This is London, you know!'

Despite her outburst on the doorstep when she mistook Emma for Susan, the old lady didn't want to talk. 'It's over and done with. I have my family to think of. Why stir up a lot of heartache? He'll have his own family now, too. I don't remember anything, anyway. I'm old and my mind is funny.'

Emma and Tyler glanced at each other and tried to sip their tea. It was a strong, orangey-coloured brew, and it was still boiling hot. If they weren't allowed to ask Vera about her wartime romance, they were at a bit of a loss to know how to proceed with the conversation.

'Tyler. What kind of name is that?' Vera asked, with a sniff. 'That's downright awful. It's like being called Roofer or Plaster-er, isn't it?'

Tyler forbore to say that 'Fitchett' was a little odd too. He smiled and told her it was a surname on his mother's side, given to him for family reasons.

'They all had funny names, though, those boys. Bobby-Jim and so on. Bobby-Jim *junior*, I beg your pardon! And Orville. Awful Orville.' Vera went into a vague little reverie of her own, thinking of the people who bore those names, presumably. Drift-ing back to a time sixty-five years ago.

They sat in Vera's little sitting room, with the bay window looking out up the street. The long row of terraced houses snaked away into the distance. Emma tried, tentatively, to ask Vera if she had a photograph of, um, the man.

'No. No photographs. No letters. No nothing.' The old lady pursed her lips, and studied Emma, who looked very crestfallen. 'You've got his hair. He had black hair just like yours.' Vera said. 'Poor Susan. I didn't want her to look like Joe.'

'Why not?'

'I thought nobody would take her if she had his looks.'

'Why? Did you think he was ugly, or something?'

'He was a dream come true, they all were, or else they were a nightmare. Someone took her then, poor little scrap?'

It was hard to picture Susan as a poor little scrap. These days she was a tall substantial woman who wore no-nonsense shirts and sensible walking shoes. When Emma had left her this morn-ing, Susan had been planning to spend the day digging over her vegetable patch, followed by a bit more spring-cleaning round at Grandpa George's house, to show that he was almost forgiven.

'Yes, George and Evelyn—my grandparents—they adored her. They were good parents to her. They didn't tell her she was adopted though; they tried to keep it a secret. That's why we'd like to find out more.'

Vera looked a little sad, and stirred her tea again.

'You'll never find GI Joe. I tried. He's gone home and good riddance.'

'So he was a soldier, ma'am?' Tyler smiled at Vera, and Emma could see that she had warmed to him, even if she didn't like his name.

'He told me he only joined up to travel. He said he didn't know where he'd get sent when they got on the ship. I think he was rather pleased it was England coz he liked the idea of seeing France—taking a look at Paris, and all that. Must have met some French girl. He liked that idea, too. I wrote to his commanding officer, but he didn't reply.'

'Where was he from, Vera?' She didn't even notice that Tyler slipped up and used her first name. She didn't seem to mind too much.

'He said he was from Lakota, but afterwards someone told me I got it wrong and he must have said 'Dakota'. That's quite a big place in America, isn't it?

Tyler nodded and leant forward to speak to her. 'Actually, he might have said Lakota.'

'Is that nearby?'

'In a manner of speaking, ma'am.'

'Well, I wasn't deaf back then, and I *thought* that's what he said.' She reflected for a moment. 'He may have said something about the Black Hills, too.'

'That would be right,' Tyler said. 'You've got a good memory, Mrs Fitchett. Now I'll bet you do remember the guy's name. It's not something you'd forget, really, is it?' he smiled at her and the dimples were having their usual effect.

For half a second Emma thought he'd done it—charmed it out of her—but instead, Vera clammed up. She was sorry, but she wouldn't say any more. She wanted the past to be dead and buried. She knew she would be dead and buried soon.

Emma wanted to ask more questions, but Tyler said it was time to go. They had to leave because it wouldn't be right to up-set an old lady who just wanted to let the past slip peacefully away.

Tyler went into thanking mode and said elaborate thank-yous all the way up the hall to the front door. 'The cup of tea was just wonderful, Mrs Fitchett. And those cakes—they were just delicious... we really appreciate all your hospitality... you've been so very kind, letting us into your lovely home, when we are just two strangers in London... so wonderful to meet a real East Ender...' The old lady even ran back for a couple more slices of cake to help sustain them on the long drive home. Tyler started thanking her all over again, and Emma rolled her eyes.

Vera's last comment was for Emma, though. She leaned in close and whispered a piece of advice. She tried to warn her off Tyler.

'Don't do it, dearie, he seems nice enough but they only want one thing.'

In the car, Emma was quiet, thinking about all the things she hadn't got the chance to ask. That woman was her grandmother, for heaven's sake. Tyler seemed to sense that all was not well.

'I'm sorry, baby. I know you need to know the truth, but we couldn't keep pushin' her. I don't know if something awful happened or what, but I'd say that lady is hurtin' pretty bad over this. Let's just give her time and try again, shall we?'

*  *  *

### April 1944

Vera heard Miranda give a stifled kind of scream, and she heard the sound of her friend's feet scrabbling on the path, trying to get away. Vera didn't get a chance to scream herself, because a hand was clamped firmly over her mouth and she was pulled aside into the trees. Her assailant was strong, and he just lifted her off her feet and carried her into the dark. He was a soldier, of course; she knew that from the familiar texture of his jacket. She also knew what she had to do. She sank her teeth into his hand, like the ferocious little alley cat she was.

'Hey! What the hell did you do that for, when I'm trying to help you out!' The man yelled at her. Vera's assailant was Joe.

'You let me go, you good-for-nothing vagabond—I can scream blue bloody murder, I can!' Vera began to demonstrate this skill, and she did indeed have a cry that would shatter bone china. Joe tried to stifle her mouth again.

'I'm not going to hurt you, you stupid girl. I'm not with the other guys,' he said, trying to keep his voice to a hoarse angry whisper.

She twisted her head free, to try to get a proper look at him. 'If you ain't going to hurt me, you let me go. I can look after myself. My friend's the one I have to worry about. Let me go, so I can get her, poor kid!'

This was not what Joe had expected and he must have released his grip just enough for her to make her move, because the next thing he knew he was nursing a bruised shin and another more painful injury between his legs.

'Miranda! Yell out so I can find yer!' Vera said, and she was blazing through the bushes like a screaming meemie looking for her friend. She hollered at the top of her lungs, and as soon as she stumbled upon someone in the dark she rained blows down on his back.

Joe followed and grabbed the man who had tackled Miranda and pushed him aside.

The offending soldier protested into the dark. 'Hey, Tony! What the hell are you doing?'

'Tony ain't here, dumb ass,' said a second voice behind him. 'Bloody Italians, letting us down.'

'Who the hell is that guy, if it ain't Tony?'

Somebody yelled 'Police!' as if they'd arrived, and a frisson of fear went through Joe, who didn't want to be up on an assault charge. Then he realised there had not been enough time for the police to get there, and it must be one of Vera's tactics.

Then somebody started waving a flashlight about, and that really caused a stir because no one wanted to get into trouble with the wardens. They didn't want to attract the Jerries' attention either. A man from one of the cottages in Lighthouse Lane came running out to see what had happened, and his dog was barking like crazy.

That was it. The boys who had planned the attack picked themselves up and fled into the darkness and the dog yapped around the small group who were left.

Lit up by the flashlight were the three who remained: Miranda, with her tearstained face, Vera, with an angry glare and smudged lipstick, and Joe, eyes sullen and wary. They looked at one another and tried to understand what had happened there in the dark.

'You alright?' Joe said to Miranda, but she was too stunned and shaken to reply. Vera stared angrily at him, frowning and out of breath. 'No thanks to you!'

The man with the dog was upon them now. 'I've seen your face now, boy, and I'll be speaking to your commanding officer.'

Miranda spoke up, sounding remarkably calm and composed. 'That won't be necessary, thank you, this soldier came to help us, when he heard our cries. The real culprits are long gone.'

'Are you sure of that, Miss?'

'Absolutely sure. My friend here will vouch for him too, won't you Vera?' She looked at Vera and waited for her to answer. There was a long pause.

'Thanks for coming out, mister, you're a hero in my book,' Vera said, and for half a second Joe looked pleased because he thought she was talking to him. Then he realised she meant the man with the half-crazed dog, and his face fell.

'You'd better put that light out, before you get us into trouble.' Miranda said.

Vera snapped the light off and they were standing in the dark again.

The man with the dog spoke. 'I'm off home, if you ladies are sure that everything is above board.' He called to his dog and turned and headed back up the path to his house.

'May I walk you home the rest of the way?' Joe said into the darkness, and there was a bit of a pause.

'Don't push your luck,' said Vera.

* * *

Back at the cottage in the little attic room, Miranda didn't stay calm for long. In fact, she just broke. She sat on the edge of the bed and cried and cried. She said she thought her nerve was gone, after all that. It was worse than when she saw the tavern go up in flames.

'Your face is a mess,' Vera said, and she went to get a rag and some antiseptic. 'But don't fret, you'll be alright in a minute.'

Miranda just sobbed and sobbed. She wasn't used to any of this. Her father was a country vicar, for heaven's sake, and he wouldn't want her in an awful situation like this, no matter how patriotic it was to do war work. 'Tomorrow I'm going home. I'll telephone my parents and they'll send me the money for the fare.'

'Tomorrow is another day, girl. Don't make up your mind now. See how you feel in the morning.' Vera dabbed at her friend's face with the damp rag.

'It didn't happen tonight, but what about tomorrow, or the night after, or the night after that.'

'You gotta toughen up, girl. Most of the boys aren't like that. They're good lads, by and large. They'll try it on, of course they will, but most of them will take no for an answer. Especially if you tell them loud and clear.'

'How can you say that, after tonight? How can you be so blasé about what's happened?'

'You don't grow up in the East End of London and not know how to take care of yourself. That's why. Now listen up, while I tell you how to deal with this kind of thing. First of all, you've got to forget all about being ladylike and learn how to scream like a stuck pig if you ever get into a mess like that again, you hear me?' Vera said. 'My dad always said that if I started screaming, they could hear me on the other side of Tower

Bridge. He always knew when his little Vera was in trouble. Another thing, girl. You've got to get yourself a good panty-girdle, you hear? One of them roll-on ones that goes down your legs a bit. Something they can't get into that easy—not without your say so. And if he don't want to take no for an answer, you've got to kick him where it hurts, right? Or you can go for his eyes—if he still don't take the hint!'

Miranda smiled weakly at her friend. 'You've got it all worked out, haven't you, Vera? I appreciate what you're trying to do, really. You've been marvellous. I just don't think I'll ever feel safe again.'

'We used to live near the Chinese markets, Miranda. There was a man there used to say to me—in your country rape is impossible—woman with skirt up run faster than man with trousers down—so it's a good thing we're in the canteen, isn't it? If we was like Rosie the Riveter we'd have to wear dungarees! There'd be no hope for us! Blow your nose and get over it, girl. We'll be alright—as long as we make good use of our womanly wiles.'

Miranda wasn't too sure about that.

# 12

## All Night Long

On the way to their hotel, Tyler and Emma had their first argument.

Emma had high hopes for their time in London. She had booked a room in a little guesthouse near Kew Gardens. It promised to be very romantic.

It turned out Tyler didn't even realise she had made the booking, and he wasn't amenable to the plan. He was flustered and taken aback. 'I thought I was driving you home tonight! We've done our sightseeing for today, Emma. We can easily drive back in the dark, the roads are good.'

'But we talked about it, you remember, and you said you wouldn't mind spending days and days exploring London with me.'

'Yes! I said *days*, Emma. I didn't say anything about spending the night! We can always drive up here again, and see some more. Didn't I make that clear?'

'No. I've booked a place for tonight, and I'm tired. I don't want to be stuck in the car for hours, and arrive home really late. I want to find somewhere to eat and go back to the hotel.'

'Emma, I don't feel right about it. We can stop for dinner, if you want, but then I think I should get you home. Your parents will be worried.'

'No, they won't. I told them we were staying the night. They recommended the guesthouse.'

His eyes went wide. He looked as if he was going to hyper-ventilate. 'You told your parents we were spending the night to-gether. In a room?'

'Yes, in a room. On a bed.' Emma couldn't credit it. 'Tyler, you don't seem like a prude. I thought this was what you wanted.'

He gave a short sigh, and looked right at her. 'Yes, it is, Emma. It's exactly what I want, but it's too soon, you under-stand. It's much too soon.'

Eventually it was agreed that they would go and have dinner, and he would think about it, although later when they were try-ing to enjoy their food, he told her that thinking about it was half the problem. Emma getting ahead of him was the other. He couldn't believe she'd 'gone behind his back' over this. It was too important to just slide into doing something that needed a lot of planning and consideration. Emma said she didn't think that romance should be planned. She liked spontaneity. Tyler said that was all very well, but she wasn't in a position to talk about spontaneity when she had planned to ambush him in London. Emma was horrified that he thought of it like that. *Ambush* was not a nice word. It almost made her want to go straight home.

After some tense negotiations and two glasses of beer, Tyler said he would go to the hotel with her, but when they got there, she would have to do things his way.

\* \* \*

**April 1944**

Vera wasn't all that surprised to see Joe sitting in the canteen on Monday night. He slipped in just before closing time and sat there pretending to read a newspaper.

Vera came over to swab down the table. 'I don't know what you're looking in there for,' she said, with a disparaging glance at the local rag. 'The real news is sitting down there in the bay.' She was referring to the ever-increasing number of vessels anchored in the little harbour, ready to take the troops across the channel.

'I'm just killing time,' he said. 'G.I. Joe, at your service, mademoiselle.'

'Move yer ruddy elbows, will ya,' she said, 'some of us would like to get home by half past nine.'

'Just let me know when you're ready, I'm walking you home.'

'Oh are ya? I can look after myself, you know. I told you that.'

'I know you can,' he said, and he smiled at her. 'I got a bruise on my shin to prove it. You wanna see?' He leant down and rolled up his khaki trouser leg. Vera inspected his war wound without a shred of remorse or sympathy. He had ugly little marks on his right hand, too. Bite marks.

'Yes, well. You didn't need to bother on my account,' she said.

'Where's your friend, the tall girl. Is she ok?

'Yes, yes. She wanted to pack it all in and go home, but they don't want people leaving the area—just in case she gives us away to the enemy, I s'pose—although if you ask me Jerry must have twigged that something's up, now that half the U.S. army is sitting here on the cliffs looking at him. So anyway, they said Miranda didn't have to do nights no more. They put her on mornings.'

'Good thing I'm here then,' he said, 'coz otherwise you'd have to walk home alone.'

'Don't be daft. The one thing I have not had since I got off the train from London, is a minute to meself. Loneliness is not a big problem for a girl round here.'

'No. I guess not. But tonight it's me that's walking you home.' He folded up his paper and left it on the table. 'You about ready to go?'

'Why would I walk home with you, when I can have my pick of all the other soldier boys.'

'Coz you like me, Vera,' he said, and he gave her a wide, wide smile.

'Oh, I see! You're ever so modest, an' all!'

'Do you have to get your coat, or something?' he said, with determination.

'I told you. *I can take care of myself.*'

She was weakening though—he could see it. 'I know you can, baby doll. But I sure would like to do it for you.'

He offered her his arm, and she took it.

* * *

Tyler was jumpy and awkward when they were alone in their hotel room and it turned out to be a difficult night. At first, he seemed determined to sleep fully clothed. He kept pretending he was cold, even though the heater was on and the room was quite cosy. He seemed most reluctant to take anything off.

'For goodness sake, you can't!' Emma said, 'you'll be so un-comfortable—and I don't really want your belt buckle and your buttons jabbing into me, either.'

He went into the bathroom and undressed in there, while Emma waited in a state of bewildered anxiety on the bed. He re-appeared in his t-shirt and his boxer shorts, and lay stiffly on the bed as if barbed wire ran right down the middle.

'I thought you Yanks were supposed to be overpaid, over-sexed and over *here*' she said, to encourage him. She pulled him towards her. They kissed, but then he drew away and looked down at her very earnestly.

'Look, I know these days it's almost expected that you leap into bed together pretty soon, but, I'm not the kinda guy who does that,' he said.

'Tyler. We are in bed.'

'Yeah, I know. That's what worries me,' he said, 'but we can just snuggle, can't we?'

'I suppose so, but surely that isn't all you want?'

'No.'

'Well, what on earth is the problem, then?' She paused, her mind raced towards some embarrassing conclusions. 'There isn't a *problem*, is there?'

'No! No way. All equipment checked and fully operational. It's about wanting it to be right. You know. The right time. The right place.'

Emma wondered if he meant she wasn't *the right person.* After what had happened to her with the fellow in Manchester, she was a bit paranoid about that.

Tyler continued. 'You seem a little confused about all these discoveries you are making about your family, too. I don't want to take advantage.'

'You don't fancy me, then.'

He gave a laugh, 'Emma, I do. I want you like mad.' He took her hand, and he placed it where she would find good hard evidence of that fact.

*He shouldn't have done that,* she thought. She'd die of frustration! She wanted to swoon in his arms and enjoy their night together. She wanted him to touch her and take her and make her feel wonderful. But it was hopeless; he was not going to change his mind.

'Why does this always happen to me?' she said quietly, after another twenty minutes of getting nowhere.

'What?'

'This kind of… rejection, I suppose.'

'It's not a rejection, honey.' His words were soft and soothing, but they still hurt.

'If it isn't, then why do I feel like this?' Her voice shook. She didn't want to cry, but she had a feeling she was going to.

'Like what?' he asked, and turned to face her.

'Like after Matthew stopped calling.' The minute the man's name was out of her mouth she knew she wouldn't be able to stop tears coming down her cheeks.

'Who?'

'Matthew, in Manchester,' she said. 'He was my—' She couldn't say anymore. The tears were coming fast, and soon she was sobbing. It was unbelievably embarrassing.

'Emma, sweetheart! Don't cry over him. I don't want you to cry!'

'I'm sorry,' she said, 'I can't help it.'

'What the hell did that guy do?' Tyler said, in confusion. 'Why are you hurting so bad over him?'

'Because I thought he loved me, and he didn't. Keen enough to begin with, of course. We were together every day for a while, *and every night,*' she said. Emma knew she shouldn't have added that, but she couldn't stop herself, she didn't care if she hurt Tyler, not now. 'And it was so good,' she continued bitterly, 'so bloody good that I thought it meant that we would always be together. I thought we were made for each other.'

She stopped and waited for Tyler's reaction, but he just carried on stroking her hair. She was surprised that he didn't push her away. He didn't say anything, so she continued. She didn't sound so angry now, just unhappy. 'But then it sort of faded out... no terrible argument or anything... I never seemed to be quite what he wanted, that's all. I still don't really understand what on earth I did wrong.'

'How could you have done anything wrong?' Tyler said, and his voice was as gentle as ever. He pulled her round to look at her face. 'Did you really think he was perfect for you, Emma? Or was there ever anything that told you he wasn't right?'

She thought very carefully about this, and then she gave a reluctant sigh. 'He said I'd look better as a blonde,' she admitted.

Tyler rolled his eyes. 'The case for the prosecution is closed.'

Emma almost let herself smile, but when she thought about how hard it had been to lose Matthew, all the feelings came flooding back, and the tears.

Tyler tried to wipe her tears away, but Emma wanted passion, not compassion.

'I just kept thinking that if I could feel like that again, like I did when I was with him, then it wouldn't hurt so much,' she said.

Tyler tilted her face up to his. He looked right into her eyes, and spoke slowly, as if that would help her to accept what he had to say. 'It's called *being on the rebound*, isn't it?'

He paused for a moment, and when he continued, his voice was softer. 'It's not how I want you to feel when you're with me.'

She didn't want to tell him he was right, so she didn't reply. She dried her eyes though, pushing the tears away with the back of her hand, trying to compose herself. She could taste the saltiness on her lips, from doing all this crying.

Tyler passed her his handkerchief, from the bedside table. 'I think we need a little more time. Listen to me, sweetheart, I want you to forget Matthew in Manchester. I don't know why he didn't stick around. Some people don't know real gold when they find it. From my point of view it's a real piece of luck that he didn't see what he had. Forget him, and never give him another thought.'

'I was hoping you'd help me to forget.'

'Yes,' he said. He moved nearer to the middle of the bed and held her in his arms, 'and I will, but not here... not yet.'

She nestled against him and hoped she wouldn't cry again. He was warm and real, and it was nice to feel his strong arms around her. She told herself to put her regrets away and take comfort in being with *this* man who lay beside her now.

'I always did love fixing things,' he said, 'and I like a challenge. I'm going to fix that broken heart for you, ok?'

\* \* \*

They spent a long hard night, not getting much sleep, just trying to keep their hands off each other.

In the morning they came down to breakfast looking sullen, with shadows under their eyes. They helped themselves to cornflakes from a glass bowl on the sideboard, and the woman who ran the B&B brought them hot coffee. She seemed to sense that all was not well.

'Didn't you get a good rest, then? Did you need that extra blanket?' she asked them, with a frowning glance at their faces, 'I do like all my guests to get a good night's sleep.'

'We were just fine, thank you, Mrs. Watkins. We spent a most restful night—very comfortable. Thank you for showing us some real British hospitality... this coffee is just wonderful... and the cornflakes, let me tell you I never tasted such excellent...' Tyler was off again. Emma couldn't listen to him. He could turn ordinary good manners into an Olympic sport.

Emma reflected on the fact that loads of other couples must have stayed in that bed upstairs, and she suspected that most of them had had a lot more fun than she had. She felt as if she was the only girl in the world who had ever been left wanting more. She couldn't *make* Tyler want to make love to her.

They drove home and hardly spoke during the journey. All the way home, Emma kept thinking about the little that Vera had been willing to tell them. Why did she say 'good riddance' and then say he was a dream come true? Or did she mean he was a nightmare? Why was she scared that Susan would look like him?

Emma felt worried that Vera might die and leave so much untold.

\* \* \*

Susan Rowland was glad when her daughter got back. She had a suspicion that it might not all be plain sailing for the young lovers. She came through from the kitchen drying her hands on her apron.

'Hello! How did it go!'

'It was okay, I suppose.' Emma's dull, disappointed tone said it all.

'Oh dear. What happened?'

'Nothing!' Emma said in frustration. 'Absolutely bloody nothing.'

'Oh.' Susan paused, looking at her daughter. 'You haven't had a fight, have you?'

'Not exactly.' Emma almost kicked her overnight bag, which she had slung down on the floor in the hall. 'Mum, I don't understand. He said he wanted to come with me, and we'd have a great time and see the sights… but all he wanted to do was buy postcards and toy beefeaters and souvenirs with union jacks on! He was quite difficult about going to the guesthouse. Horrible, in fact. I don't understand. I thought he wanted to be with me!'

'Give the boy a chance. It's probably best not to rush into anything. Tyler seems to have a lot of good qualities.'

'Yes, yes,' Emma said with resignation in her voice, 'he's very gentlemanly. He insisted on paying for everything even though that means he won't have enough money to buy a car for ages. He was ever so polite, everywhere we went. Irritatingly polite, in fact. Everyone loves him, everywhere we go. They just love Tyler. He could start a fan club.'

Susan laughed and squeezed her daughter's hand.

'I have some news of my own, Emma. I have sent away a sample of my DNA to be tested. I read about it in a magazine about tracing your ancestry. Apparently it can be very revealing.'

'You are having a DNA test done? You?

'Yes. It can tell you all about your ethnic background.'

Emma looked sceptical. 'Mum, what on earth is the point? What are you hoping it will tell you?'

'Something. I hope it will tell me SOMETHING,' she said. 'I just got so sick of not being able to know what really happened.'

'But Mum—DNA can't tell us that either. The information you get from those tests is vague, it only tells you what part of the world your *distant* ancestors were from. It can't tell us his name, can it? It's so annoying that Vera won't say. I almost thought Tyler had charmed it out of her yesterday, but -'

'VERA?' Susan said, with a stricken look on her face.

'Yes. I have to tell you, Mum. I saw Vera.'

'You went to London to see Vera? Without consulting me!'

'I always planned to tell you as soon as I got home.'

'So that was the whole purpose of the trip?'

'More or less,' Emma admitted. Actually, getting Tyler into bed had been a big part of it, although not exactly a resounding success.

'But Emma, you broke the code of conduct, set out by my support group! And what about breaking my trust! Did you stop to think about that? You took it upon yourself to go there, without my permission, and…' she stopped, and bit her lip. She leant forward and looked straight at Emma. 'What was she like? Tell me everything.'

* * *

### April 1944

Tuesday night Joe was there again, and Vera didn't make such a fuss. On the way home she asked him why he joined up and he said it was the chance to travel. He liked the idea of seeing a bit of the world while he was young. Vera said she'd never been young. Nobody was born yesterday in the East End of London. If you didn't grow up fast, you didn't get to grow up at all.

Wednesday night he told her all the best ways he knew to catch fish. Vera told him not to brag and said she didn't want to listen unless he caught one for her. She was missing her mum's cod's head soup.

Thursday night he gave her a parcel wrapped in a few sheets of newspaper.

'Don't I get no chips with that, then?' she said, as she un-wrapped the fish. Joe smiled and said it was a tall order trying to please a little lady like her. He hoped the fish was good eating.

'It will be,' Vera told him, 'and I expect my landlady will be pleased.'

He reached inside his jacket pocket. 'Here, I've got you some chocolate, too. It's melted a bit.'

'Trying to sweeten me up are you?'

'You're sweet enough already, baby. Take it. No strings attached.'

Each night when they reached the gate of the cottage, she wondered what he would say or do, but all he ever did was touch his hat and turn to walk home.

Friday night came, and they stood at the gate. He put his hand on the latch to unhook it for her.

'Goodnight, Vera,' he said. 'See you Monday.' Then he tipped his hat like he always did.

That's when she grabbed his lapels and pulled him towards her.

'I s'pose I'll have to give you something,' she said, 'for your trouble.'

So she gave him a kiss, and he must have been pleased, because he gave as good as he got.

'My favourite,' he said, with a bit of a grin, and he turned to go back to his camp.

\* \* \*

At the airbase, Tyler spent his shift working on a tricky mechanical problem with one of the supply planes. His overalls were grubby and it was hot working crouched beside the plane. He eased one of his long legs into a better position. He knew he had to concentrate, a mistake could mean that the landing gear would fail, and that would be bad, but his mind kept going over what had happened with Emma. And what hadn't happened.

Bradley walked by, holding a cup of coffee in a Styrofoam mug. 'Hey, Robinson! How was your dirty weekend?'

Tyler didn't bother to look up, he was trying to force a casing open with a spanner, putting all his strength into it, hoping the nut would eventually give way. 'There was nothing dirty about my weekend, Brad.'

'No? All very beautiful and fulfilling, was it?'

Tyler channelled his anger into his work and the spanner slipped and dented the casing. 'Now look what you made me do!' He swore like a sailor and threw the spanner clanging across the workshop floor.

'Wahoo! Would you look at that, everybody!' Bradley shouted in triumph, 'Choirboy's finally lost it!'

At the other end of the shop, a crew of guys looked up and had a laugh, but they were soon busy again with their own work.

'I haven't lost it, that's the problem,' Tyler muttered under his breath, with an angry sigh. He rubbed a hand over his face in anxiety and left a big streak of oil across his forehead. 'So much for being good at fixing things! That's wrecked now; the whole casing will have to be replaced. I give up. I'm taking a break.' He got up and stalked out towards the hangar doors.

It was light and sunny outside, and the English air was cool and fresh. Nice. Peaceful. Or it would have been if Brad hadn't followed him outside to carry on baiting him.

Instead, Brad offered him a cigarette.

Tyler shook his head, and folded his arms defensively.

Brad shrugged. 'Sorry, I forgot. Clean-living Robinson doesn't do that kind of thing. Although I notice you like a beer these days, don't you? And I thought you were getting a taste for some of life's *other* pleasures too, now that you got that dusky little sweetheart of yours.'

Tyler gave a short sigh, and put his oily hand back over his face.

'Buddy,' Brad began, suppressing a laugh, 'you are going to look like a black and white minstrel if you don't stop doing that.'

'To hell with it.'

Brad frowned. 'You didn't have such a good weekend, did you?'

'No.' Tyler knew he sounded melancholy. It gave his friend the clue he needed.

'You didn't take her all the way to London and NOT get it on with her, did you?' Brad said, incredulously. 'Tell me you didn't do that?'

Tyler didn't reply, but the look on his face gave away the answer.

'You did!' Brad gave a great belly laugh and punched him on the arm. 'Come on! You think all she wants is holding hands and sweet nothings? I'm surprised she's even speaking to you!'

'So am I.'

'Jeez, how could you DO that, Tyler? She's hot. With those cherry lips of hers and that long dark hair—she could give a man a night to remember, I'll bet. What's wrong with you? I'd have had her over and over again!'

'STOP!' Tyler said. This was unbearable. 'Don't say that. You don't know me. You don't know her. You don't understand ANYTHING!'

'I understand that getting close to her scares the hell out of you,' Brad said.

Tyler looked across at him sharply. Brad wasn't normally the one to hit the nail on the head, not where women were concerned. Flashes of unexpected insight were a whole new development.

Brad was onto something now, and it got worse. 'Is it because we're only here until September? You'll have to say goodbye to her then, unless you're dumb enough to try and take her home with you. Or is that the problem? Mom and Dad might not like your taste in souvenirs?'

Tyler didn't like what Brad was implying. 'My parents might have some reservations about Emma, but I do assure you they are not—' Then he stopped. He didn't want to say what they were not, because maybe they were.

'Reservations, eh?' Brad chuckled. 'That's for sure. Well, you can have a good time with her now, and then forget all about her and go back home and date the girl next door, can't you? It's your life.'

It all sounded so easy, but it wasn't the way Tyler worked. He frowned and gazed out in the direction of the runway. 'It's more complicated than that.'

But Brad was tired of this, he didn't believe in doing a lot of soul-searching. 'Come on; stop moping around out here like a lovesick puppy. Why don't I help you get that casing off, Tyler, before we have to file a report for loss of efficiency? We don't want to do that, do we?'

# 13

# Needle in the Haystack

Tyler knew that Emma was disappointed—firstly about Vera clamming up, and secondly because of lack of action with him. He wanted to redeem himself with her.

They sat in the garden at the cottage, enjoying some weak English sunshine, and the first summer roses that climbed over the arbour. Keith had sent them out there, indicating that they should try out the rustic little bench in the arbour. He called it 'the love seat'—to Emma's acute embarrassment.

Tyler was making the best of it, and he put his arm around his girl. 'Cheer up, sweetheart, summer's really coming now, isn't it? It's no time to be sad.'

'I wanted to know his name, that's all. Vera could so easily have told us.'

'What if she *has* told us his name, Emma? She kept calling him Joe.'

'She said G.I. Joe, that's all.'

'What if he really was called Joe? Some of them must have been given that name.'

'Tyler. There were over a million G.I.s stationed in Britain. More than million. I should think quite a few of them were named Joe. But probably not the man that Vera knew.' Emma sighed. 'It is so infuriating. She should just tell us. My mother has a right to know.'

'Your mum does have a right to know,' Tyler said, 'I've always thought so, but lately I have noticed that *you* seem to be more obsessed about finding out the truth than she does. Your mom seems to be taking it a bit more calmly now.'

Emma picked at a splinter of wood on the armrest nearest to her. 'There's a terrible old music hall joke where the first man says 'I'm going to tell your father you did that,' and the second man gets a laugh by saying 'you'll be lucky—my father was some soldiers!' It was the kind of thing that passed for humour in the days when innuendo was all you got. I don't want to think that about my grandfather like that for the rest of my life. *I want to know his name.*'

Tyler squeezed her arm. 'I'll try to help you track him down, I promise.'

'It's impossible. There are too many of them. Without a surname it's hopeless. Loads of them had British girlfriends, you know.'

'I can understand the attraction,' Tyler said, and he gave her a grin. 'Besides. It's just a fact of life. Wherever there are soldiers, there are sweethearts, and where there are sweethearts, there are… consequences.'

'I suppose they didn't have condoms back then?' Emma said, almost to herself, and then realised that she'd spoken out loud.

'They did have them,' Tyler said. 'The army issued them in their thousands. Prophylactics, they called them. A lot of the boys didn't wear them. Some for religious reasons. Some just didn't want to. Apparently some of the men used them for other purposes—like they would put their wristwatch in 'em and tie it up—to try to keep it dry when they were in the transports going over to Normandy.'

She turned and looked at him. 'You seem remarkably well informed. How on earth did you know all that?'

'I mighta googled it,' Tyler admitted.

'You googled World War Two condoms?
'Yeah.'

'Do you usually look at that kind of thing on the internet?'

'No. Emma. Not at all! It was only because of all this, you know, because you wanted to know—'

The blush spread across his face like red wine spilt on a tablecloth.

'You did it for me?' Emma said, hoping to help him off the hook.

'Yeah.'

'That's really very sweet of you. Thank you.'

He coughed and tried to compose himself, endeavouring to recover a bit of his dignity. 'The point is, Emma—' He hesitated in another blaze of blushing scarlet.

'Yes?' She said, and waited for him. She smiled. 'Is this point coming, or not?'

'The point is that the problem of tracking Joe down, is a matter of mathematics—a question of probability, to be precise. Yes, there are too many people called Joseph, I should think, but what if we find someone called Joseph who enlisted from Dakota, and what if we find him in the same unit as someone called Orville? Now it's getting more interesting, isn't it? And then, just suppose we find Bobby-Jim in the same crew of guys. And, they all have to be stationed here in Devon, in 1944, and not just anywhere round here, but here in this town. I think there's a good chance we can find him, Emma.'

* * *

*May 1944*

Joe took Vera to a 'Dine and Dance' at the hotel. Joe said he liked to dance and he reckoned she liked it too. Vera said she was only going for the dinner. Joe said that if that was the case, she was out of luck. If she really wanted a good meal she should come back and dine with him at the camp. The hotel only had two main dishes on the menu: omelette (made with powdered egg), and sausages in gravy (and no animals were harmed in the making).

'Spoilt for choice!' she told him, and squeezed his arm.

There were quite a few other servicemen there that day, along with a few of the locals. Joe and Vera shuffled around the dance floor to a slow sentimental song about a boy in khaki, and a girl in lace. Joe held her close and told her he was crazy about her. Vera whispered back that she knew what his game was and not to get his hopes up.

They were surprised to see Miranda, sitting at one of the other tables, waiting for her beau. She waved at them to come over, and insisted that they sit down and join her. She'd cut her hair. She looked good with the Hollywood curls.

'Did you find yourself an officer, then?' Joe enquired, although he knew it was less than polite. Miranda blushed.

Vera laughed. 'No, you dimwit. Officers don't come in that colour.' She nodded her head at Miranda's boyfriend, who was standing over by the bar. He was an African American and he flashed them an extravagant smile.

'Black as the night sky over Croydon,' Vera observed. 'I'm surprised you don't lose him in the bedclothes, after you've blown the candle out.'

'I just ask him to give me a grin,' Miranda said, with a laugh.

'She's come out of her shell a bit, hasn't she!' Vera said, and she prodded at Joe, who was looking a trifle surprised. He didn't say anything.

In actual fact, it was Vera and Miranda who had to share a bed, due to overcrowding in a town overflowing with extra people. Their landlady was not at all amenable to visits from handsome black soldier boys. It wasn't easy for Miranda, but she just smiled a sweet, dreamy smile, and looked at her guy standing by the bar. 'I adore him. He makes me feel safe.'

'That's what you think!' Vera said. 'Anyway, none of us is safe here, these days. Did you hear them bombers come over last night?'

Miranda's young man came back with the drinks and they talked about places they knew that had been bombed. There was a lot of terse comment about never knowing when your number was up. Cigarettes were passed round and people pulled on them gratefully and blew smoke across the room in the direction of the dance floor.

'Don't look now, Miranda, but there's trouble lurking right beside us,' Vera said, with the merest inclination of her head, 'that lot keep giving your bloke the evil eye.'

On the adjacent table was a group of young men from the South, and they didn't take kindly to seeing a young black man with a girl like Miranda. They started making nasty comments. Miranda's young man made no reaction, except to lean across the table and take his sweetheart's hand. 'Honey, I don't want no trouble. There are plenty of places we can go for a drink.' Miranda's pale slender fingers looked very white indeed with his sturdy brown hands around them.

'If you think so, darling, I do so want to enjoy the evening,' she said, and she reached for her beaded evening bag. 'I hear they have quite a nice bar at the Horse and Plough.'

'Sit down and drink the one you've already paid for,' Vera said, and she turned to glower at the other young men. 'I don't know what you're all staring at,' she said, in a loud voice. 'He ain't fighting on Hitler's side, is he? You save your ill manners for him. You can shut your traps and all.'

Joe looked up when she said that. 'Baby doll, you got such a sweet way of making your point!'

* * *

Helen wanted to know why Emma didn't want to go out dancing any more. Helen had even started going to classes, to learn a few moves. Partner dancing wasn't so bad after all. She wanted Emma to come along and give her a bit of moral support.

'Too busy,' Emma said, with a hint of guilt, she knew she'd been neglecting her best friend. 'I just want to be with Tyler.'

'You could bring Tyler with you. You say he's a good dancer. We need some extra men.'

'Yeah. I could. He's even offered, it's just that—'

'Oh, I see,' Helen said, with a wry laugh. 'You don't want to
*share* him. Must be serious!'

# 14

# The Air Show

Tyler told them the base was doing a big Air Show on Saturday, and invited them all along. He said he'd be really honoured if they showed up, and it would be almost as nice as having his own family there. Sometimes he felt like the Rowlands had become his second family.

Keith was quite keen to see the show, and Susan agreed to go because there was just a chance she might glean some more information about the war. The air base had been a hive of activity during the forties.

Emma promised they'd all be there.

She had dropped Tyler off at the Air Base quite a few times, but she'd never been inside it before. Today, it was hot and there was a long queue of cars on the approach road that led to the base. They inched along in the family car, slowly getting closer to the huge sign with the Eagle on it.

'Is this the base they call the Eagles' Nest?' Keith asked, as they edged forward towards the barrier.

'No. That would be RAF Lakenheath. That's where the Eagles are—the F15s,' Emma explained, newly knowledgeable about all this stuff since she met Tyler. 'But you won't be disappointed, Dad. Tyler said the Eagles are going to do a flypast.'

'Well, that'll be a sight to see.'

'Keith.' Susan was using her matron-giving-a-warning tone of voice. 'You know how I feel about displays of military might, don't you? And as for all these gruff ideas about 'maintaining supremacy' and all that—don't even let me get started!'

'Of course, of course.' Keith wasn't likely to forget his wife's ardent pacifist feelings.

'Mum—you're not going to be wearing your woolly peacenik hat the whole day, are you?' Emma said. She had a nightmare vision of her mother standing on a soapbox on the parade ground shouting at everyone, or sneaking into a fighter plane to sabotage its important bits. 'You promise you won't embarrass me, or Tyler, or anyone.'

'I shall be a model parent, Emma.'

'He's important to me, Mum.'

'I know. That's what worries me.'

The whole thing had been 'organised' to within an inch of its life, and there were soldiers everywhere explaining what they had to do. There were orange cones and signposts and paths laid out for the stream of vehicles that led into the base. Keith lowered his window to speak to a smart young man in uniform, and he directed them into a neighbouring field where they could leave their car.

'Marshals will show you exactly where to park, sir.'

'I bet they will. Thank you!'

They followed the hordes of people who were all walking across the grass in the direction of the airfield. There was quite a crowd on the tarmac over by some low grey buildings. That seemed to be the scene of the action.

'Will we get the chance to say hello to Tyler, do you think?'

'He's on the static display, in Hangar number 16,' Emma said.

'Later on we'll go and find him,' said Keith, 'I'd love to see the static, anyway. You don't get many chances to see fighter planes up close—not these days.' He gave a wary glance at his wife, but she was reading the programme of planned events.

Emma took her father's arm. 'I'll make sure you get to see the planes, Dad. That's what we're here for. It's going to be spectacular. The weather's perfect, for a start. I'm going to enjoy every minute of it, and Tyler said he'd try to find us when he's on a break.'

There was a flypast of military planes, which wowed the crowd, and an aerobatics demonstration. The planes roared overhead and left bright streams of colour in the air. There was a running commentary but the noise of the airplanes drowned most of it out. Parachutes fluttered down onto a grassy expanse beyond the airstrip, and each expert landing brought fresh applause from the cheering onlookers. The highlight of the afternoon was when they saw the War Birds—Hurricanes and Spitfires roaring across the sky, just as they did in the 1940s. Keith read out a little piece in the programme about the American contribution to the war, and Susan found herself feeling a little tearful.

'Oh look, there's Tyler!' Emma said, as she saw him coming towards them through the crowd. She waved and so did he. She thought he looked fantastic in his formal uniform—a vision in Air Force blue—and she really liked the way the smartly tailored jacket emphasized his shoulders. He came and stood with them and told them it was all going just fine. His commanding officer was very pleased about the numbers. The base was full of people.

'This beautiful weather has done us a favour,' Tyler said. 'Would you look at that clear blue sky!'

Emma didn't want to look at the sky—not when she could look at Tyler. She just wanted to drink him in so that she would always remember the way he looked today, tall and handsome in his military finery.

'Didn't I do up all my buttons, or something?' he said, when he saw her staring.

'No. Everything is just perfect,' she said, in a small quiet voice.

Keith and Susan exchanged a knowing look. Emma saw it and forced herself to concentrate on the entertainment on the parade ground.

There was a big contingent of soldiers in a brass band, and an impressive display of marching. The men and women stamped up and down with energy and precision in every step.

After a whole selection of military marches, the guys delighted the crowd with a medley from the Glenn Miller Band. There were cheers and a smatter of applause as the familiar sounds flooded the airfield.

'Don't you just love that old time stuff,' Tyler said, with his hand on Emma's back. She could almost feel his body moving in time to the beat. With the sun on her face and her handsome young airman by her side she felt so happy.

'Yes, it's great,' she said, and her feet were itching to join in with the rhythm.

'Puts me *in the mood*, that's for sure,' Tyler said, and he grinned. Then he cast a respectful glance at Mr and Mrs Rowland. 'For dancing,' he added, with a blush.

'Are you going to give us a demonstration?' Keith chipped in, not very seriously. 'Emma tells us you're a champion dancer.'

Emma knew that Tyler wouldn't understand Keith's use of the word 'champion' in that sentence.

'I wouldn't say that, Mr Rowland, I'm just a keen beginner, really,' Tyler said, 'and I would love to give Emma a dance, but I'm in uniform, and I mustn't do anything inappropriate while I'm in uniform.' Tyler straightened up when he said that, and Susan stepped out of his way in case he felt the need to salute.

Emma reflected that he didn't loosen up all that much when he wasn't in his uniform, either. Susan gave her a sympathetic smile.

'Well, may I suggest that we go in search of an ice cream, or an *American hot dog*,' Susan said, with a sideways glance at Tyler, 'if that's what takes your fancy!'

Emma wanted to kick her in the shins but she decided it would only encourage her. They went in search of some lunch.

Afterwards, she walked back to Hangar 16 with Tyler. He glanced about and gave her a furtive little kiss and then he went back to his post. There was an old Lancaster bomber on display and Tyler was stationed just beside the steps leading up to the hatch. There was a whole queue of people needing to be helped in and out of the airplane, plenty to keep him busy for the next few hours. He nodded and smiled at each and every one of them as they passed by. Emma left him to it and began to walk away. A stout woman in her fifties leant heavily on Tyler as she got out of the plane. 'Are you a pilot, dear?' Emma heard her say.

'No, ma'am,' Tyler replied, 'for every person in the air there are a hundred on the ground, you know.'

Emma smiled. He'd get to say that a few times today. What she loved about him, though, was that every time he said it he sounded so sweet and so polite. So full of fresh enthusiasm.

That was when it hit her. *I'm in love with him,* she realised. *I am. I know I am. Mum, Dad, where have you gone? Wait! Don't let this happen to me. Not again.* She walked out of the hangar with her head in a whirl. *It's too late, isn't it? I'm in love with him.*

She realised that it didn't matter what happened with him now. Maybe they'd get it together, maybe they wouldn't. It made no difference now, and it gave her a rising sense of panic. All possible outcomes seemed likely to lead to getting hurt.

Keith and Susan were immersing themselves in the history of wartime Britain, in the next hangar. There was a big sign up that said 'Operation Overlord', and a display of photographs about what the base was like during the war. Apparently it was a monumental task getting enough men and equipment across the Channel to make the invasion a success in 1944. The man on the stand was talking them through it.

'Over a hundred and fifty thousand men, you say, and all those weapons and equipment?'

'Yes. It was a mighty big operation, sir.'

'And it all happened from here, in sleepy little towns like ours, along the South coast?' Susan was trying to take it all in.

'Yes, ma'am. It's hard to imagine it now, but I believe it had a big impact on people in Britain at the time.'

'Oh, it left its mark, alright,' Susan said ruefully. Keith squeezed her hand. Then he spoke to his daughter, who had joined them.

'Emma—there you are! Come and have a look at this. You wanted to know how many soldiers were stationed near us, didn't you, love?'

Emma did want to know, even though her head was in a whirl. One of those men was her grandfather. The person in charge of the display scrutinised his map of the bay near where the Rowlands lived.

'I'd say about twenty thousand of our guys left from there,' he said.

'Well that narrows it down quite a bit.' Keith almost laughed, except that his wife's face told him this was no joke. Emma didn't look all that amused either.

'Emma, poppet, are you alright?' Keith said, and looked anxiously at her.

'I think I'd like to go home now, she said. 'Can I go and wait in the car? I've seen enough of all this military stuff.' Emma turned to go.

'Really? I thought you were rather taken with it,' Keith said in confusion, but she was already walking away.

'She is.' Susan touched her husband's arm. 'Scary thought, isn't it? All this talk of threats and deterrents and strike forces. All this power over life and death. Imagine how awful it would be if it took Tyler away from her?'

\* \* \*

## May 1944

Vera's attic room in the house on the headland commanded a very good view of the bay. From that vantage point, she was well informed about the preparations. Every day the bay was full of vessels, and from up here they looked like lead-coloured toys bobbing about. They seemed so out of place in the pretty little harbour. It was a holiday resort, a place for fun and games on the beach and leisurely walks down the pier—not lining up battle-ships ready for war.

At night they took them further out, so they would be less vulnerable to attack, but during the day there they were, for all to see. Vera turned away from the window, checked her hair and her lipstick and went downstairs to open the door.

Joe was standing there, cap in hand.

'Will you go on a picnic with me, Vera? Tomorrow? We could walk out somewhere nice.'

She hesitated. It was not her Standard Operating Procedure to go anywhere too far away from other people. You never knew when you might need to sound the alarm.

Joe was persuasive. 'I'll bring the food, of course,' he said.

'Yes, well, I was just thinking that my landlady's got a hamper, but I haven't got a clue what you expect me to put in it. Smoked salmon and caviar, maybe. Champagne ham and pine-apple, perchance?'

'You'll come then, Vera?'

'I s'pose so, Joe. Don't go getting all soppy with me, though. I can't afford to get fond of you. You'll be off soon, by the look of it.'

'Yeah,' he said. 'I just got assigned to a rifle company.'

'Oh my gawd, Joe. A rifle company!' Her hands flew up to her face, and she covered her mouth. Her eyes were wide with fear. Sky blue eyes with tears coming, fast.

'I knew you liked me, Vera. I knew all along.' He broke into a slow smile.

'Is there any way you can get out of it?'

'No, Vera, of course not. I got a job to do.'

'You could have done your job with another unit, couldn't you? Can't you get them to put you with quartermaster in charge of supplies, or something like that?'

'I guess they'll have more need of me with the rifle company. I'll pick you up tomorrow, same time.'

'Wait, Joe, wait.' She pulled him into a tearful embrace, and they kissed for a few moments. Then she forced herself to consider their plans for tomorrow. 'If you're bringing the food, what do you want me to bring?'

'Just yourself,' he said, and glanced across the bay.

She knew he was hoping she'd provide the entertainment. Question was, would she be wearing that ironclad girdle of hers, or would she forget about that, this time?

# 15

## Probability

That night, in the cosy little sitting room in the Rowlands' cottage, Tyler outlined their plan of attack. They would search the Enlistment Records online. He promised Susan he'd find the name of her father by the end of the evening, or at the very least give her a shortlist of possible suspects. Susan was more than a little sceptical.

'I can't share your ridiculous optimism, dear boy. It says there are nine million soldiers listed on this website. To me it looks hopeless, far worse than hunting for a needle in a haystack.'

'That's where computers are so great, though, isn't it, Mrs Rowland? You see, I just open up the database that gives all the soldier's names, and I can run my searches through it quite quickly.'

'Watch and learn, Mum, watch and learn.' Emma said, and she and Tyler put their heads close together to look at the screen. Emma thought they could have done all this upstairs in her bedroom, where they wouldn't be disturbed by the telly, but of course, Tyler said that might be *inappropriate*. Emma had become rather accustomed to hearing that word.

Tyler said they should tackle the problem systematically, and he had drawn up a number of charts. He had included every unit that was stationed in the vicinity, and a few that were really too far away, with blank spaces alongside so they could tick them off as they eliminated them from their enquiries.

'I reckon we should look for Orville first, as that's quite an unusual name. Each time we locate an Orville we check the rest of the unit to see if we can find Bobby-Jim, who will be listed as 'Robert James', I would guess.' His fingers typed the search term in and they all waited around with bated breath.

Keith said it was surprising how many Orvilles there were.

'Now comes the hard part,' said Tyler, 'we have to double check for Bobby Jim. This could take a while.'

'It's a good game played slow, isn't it?' Susan said wryly.

'Lots of things are like that,' Emma said, under her breath. She was still smarting from Tyler's dogged determination to avoid being alone with her.

After a while Susan got sick of looking over Emma's shoulder to see if they'd found anything. They were still miles away from Joe, by the look of it. She nudged Keith and said they might pop down to the pub for a drink and leave the youngsters to it. Emma's mood brightened, instantly. She practically shooed them out of the door.

Tyler fiddled nervously with his lists and furrowed his brow in concentration.

As soon as they were alone Emma came and sat beside him again, and stroked his cheek to get his attention. 'We could take a break, you know. We don't have to keep at it all night.' Emma glanced over in the direction of the couch.

He frowned and his young face looked troubled. 'No, I don't think so, Emma. What if we were getting all steamed up on the couch and your parents walked in on us?'

'They won't. That's what they've gone out for! To give us time together.'

'But we are together, honey.' He stroked the side of her face, and then he relented and gave her an arousing kiss. A long, hard, aching kiss. She could feel his desire for her, she could taste it, but she knew he would break away and he did. 'You know, it's still a little soon for third base, don't you think?'

Emma looked at him with a cool, level gaze. 'Tell me, Tyler, what exactly does it mean—to get to third base?'

He blushed. 'You know what it means.'

'I don't have a clue,' she said, innocently, 'I don't know a thing about baseball. It was not part of my education. You'll have to explain it to me.'

'It hasn't got that much to do with baseball.'

'I realise that, you idiot. But make the parallel, explain it to me.' She folded her arms and gave him a demanding stare.

He frowned. He didn't believe in discussing these things. Some things shouldn't have to be said—not by him, anyway. He coughed. 'My understanding of it is that first base is like kissin' and stuff. Well, mainly just kissin' and not so much stuff. Second base is... um... above the waist activity, you know, with clothes on... and third base would be... any other activity... below...' he stopped. 'Please, Emma, don't make me say this!' He was crimson with embarrassment.

She regretted what she'd done. 'I'm sorry.'

'It's okay.'

'I don't understand,' she said. 'When we're dancing, you always seem so keen.'

'My parents always said that the dancing wasn't a good idea. To me it seemed like a great way to get close to a woman without it being improper, you understand. I love dancing.'

Emma wished and wished he'd said that he loved *her*. She dare not push him though; she was too scared of losing him.

After that they both concentrated very hard on searching for the names on the database. Three hours and twenty minutes later, Tyler struck gold.

'That'll be them! Look! There's Robert James, just there, and in the same group of infantrymen there's an Orville. Awful Orville the old lady called him. They were stationed just down the road from here, too.'

'But we need to get a hat trick, don't we?' Emma said. 'We need to find Joe in the same unit, or platoon, or whatever you call it.'

'Yeah,' Tyler's face clouded, because he'd already looked and Joe was nowhere to be seen.

'He wasn't called Joe, really, was he? That's just what they called them all. Like the Brits were called Tommy and the Germans were the Jerries. It was stupid to think he was actually called Joe.'

'He was, sugar, I'm *sure* he was. The way she said that about the child—'I didn't want her to look like Joe'—it seemed like she was using his real name. You know, these databases aren't always complete. I want to see if there's a way we can get in touch with the veterans from this company, maybe we can find out if there *was* anyone called Joe, in this group.'

'It's not his real name, Tyler.' Emma was dispirited. She had wanted to know his name.

'Well, suppose it isn't? Maybe it's a nickname, then. If we get in touch with the vets, maybe someone will know if Orville and Bobby Jim had a mate known as Joe.'

'They were all called Joe.' She sounded sad. Tyler touched her hand.

'We have to follow this up, or we'll never know.'

* * *

That night they watched a couple of old war films that Tyler rented on DVD. Emma felt terrible watching the scenes where the men keep getting gunned down trying to cross the beach. It's one thing to watch a film and follow the story. It's quite another to think of Joe being there, up to his waist in water and scared for his life, in a hail of machine gun fire. She clutched a cushion first of all, and then she changed her mind and buried her face against Tyler's rather nice chest.

'We don't have to watch this, sweetie,' he said, and he put a hand through her hair.

'We do. I want to know. I want to know what happened.'

She looked up just in time to see another group of men being gunned down in the water. 'Oh, Tyler, is that how he died?'

# 16

## The Eyewitness

There were two hundred men in the group where Tyler found awful Orville and his buddy, Bobby-Jim, neither of whom had survived the war. Their names were listed among those who fell. Tyler wondered just how many of them got to go home. There was a very high turnover in rifle companies.

Tyler sent a lot of emails and finally they tracked down a veterans' association. Tyler was thrilled when he finally got given the name of a man who had seen action on June 6th—D-day. His name was Bill and he lived in a place called Silver Springs in the state of Maryland. A very special phone call was set up so that they could talk to him.

The conference call was to be received in the Rowlands' little sitting room. Keith and Susan were going to be there, since it was such a big thing to hear an eyewitness account. Tyler and Emma set up a speakerphone on the coffee table so they could all hear his voice and listen to his story.

Tyler was detailed to ask the questions, since he 'knew the lingo' and would have less trouble making himself understood. After all, Bill was a countryman of his. Tyler was very much in awe of the fact that Bill had been in one of the first waves of men to get landed on the beach in Normandy. Tyler spent the first few moments going on and on about what an honour and a privilege it was to talk to someone who had seen action on that historic day. Emma jabbed his leg because she wanted him to get on with it. Tyler checked his list of questions and asked Bill if the fighting was bitter.

'We had some casualties,' Bill said, 'we lost a few boys on the beach, but I think it was far worse further along, did you hear about the West Virginian boys, the 115th—their casualty rate was 96 percent.'

'Yes, sir, I read about that.' Tyler said. 'It's a sobering thought.'

Bill's mind wandered away from the matter in hand. His voice cracked and warbled as he spoke. 'And you are in the security forces, yourself, did you say?'

'Yes, I'm with the air force, keeping everything ready in case anything happens in the European Theater. God forbid that it should.'

'Are you a pilot, young man?'

'No, sir. These days, for every man in the sky there are a hundred on the ground. I shouldn't say *man* in the sky either. We got lots of women pilots now.'

Emma was getting impatient, but Tyler worked his usual magic and Bill was soon ready to tell them what he remembered. He spoke about being in one of the landing craft that took the boys right up to the Normandy beaches.

'Not quite far enough, in our case. I think the guy who was in charge of the landing craft got scared. They were firing on the beach so he told us we were near enough—I reckon he was desperate to turn around and get out of there. He said we'd arrived and told us we could hop out now... we were lucky, because we didn't get blown up, but we were unlucky because we had to swim to shore from there. Honestly, I think some of the guys just drowned under the weight of all the stuff they had to carry.

'I took off my pack and let it sink, before I did. It's probably still down there somewhere. I reckoned my best chance was if I kept moving, and used whatever I could for cover. I sure was glad to crawl up onto dry land, except that I feared I was a better target once I was up out of the water… Once we had secured the beachhead, we tried to regroup and see who had made it.'

Tyler took that opportunity to ask if Bill remembered a man called Joe, from Dakota.

Bill did have a feeling there was a Joe with their company, but perhaps not in his unit. Tyler squeezed Emma's hand and looked triumphant.

'I reckon he had another name—a nickname,' Bill continued, the ancient rusty cogs in his mind struggling to turn and to re-member. 'A lot of the guys had nicknames. I don't really know if I can tell you for sure. I'll go through everything I've got here, all my old photos and memorabilia, and see what I can lay my hands on that might help you out…'

Emma looked disappointed. It sounded as if Bill was about to ring off. Susan bit her lip too. The old man would be gone in a second and he hadn't really told them anything that shed any light on Joe's fate.

'What a minute, you don't mean Chief, do you? He was from Dakota. I can't be sure, but I think his Christian name was Joseph. I could be wrong of course—we always called him Chief.'

'That'll be him, I reckon.' Tyler said, and he held onto Emma's hand in a hopeful expectation. 'What was he like?'

'Oh, he was well liked. Everyone felt a little safer with him around. He was only a private, mind you, but the guys respected him.'

'Did he make it off the beach, Bill?' Tyler said. Emma listened intently. This was the question she had been longing for Tyler to ask, concerning that issue, at least. It was the one thing she most wanted to know.

'I think he might have, if this is the same guy we're talking about. Although I'd say he did his best to get himself killed.'

'Oh no, Bill,' said Emma, 'did he not fight bravely, then? Did he feel suicidal or something?' She realised she didn't want to hear any bad of him. She'd kind of got to like old Joe. She tried to check her feelings, and she braced herself to hear what he was really like. 'Please Bill, tell me what you know, I want to hear it all. Don't hide anything, if you think he was a coward, just tell me.'

'Well, he never fired a gun in anger, I can tell you that much,' Bill said, and there was a sound a bit like a chuckle. 'That guy wasn't a coward, though, he was a medic.'

'A medic!' Emma looked at Tyler and Tyler looked at her. That would explain why he wasn't listed with the other guys, maybe. It would explain quite a few things, in fact.

'Bill, can you tell us what you mean when you say he tried hard enough to get himself killed? Can you tell us about that, sir?'

'Well, if he's the guy I have in mind, he kept running back into the water to get more men to safety. He was a good swimmer, you see, and he couldn't stand by and see a man drown just because he got shot in the arm or something. Not when he reckoned he could do something for them. He had no formal medical training—except what the army gave him—but when it came to it those boys got a lot of respect—they often got called 'Doc', because of what they could do to save lives. To us, he was more than just the medicine man.'

'That would figure,' Tyler said.

Emma knew it was a long shot, but she had to ask. 'Bill, listen. Do you know if that guy had a girlfriend called Vera?

'Honey, its been sixty-five years, you know! I have the utmost difficulty recalling the names of my *own* girlfriends let alone anyone else's.'

Susan looked away. She'd always known that her 'birth father' was probably a fly-by-night—but it was hard to hear, all the same.

'Your mom's story doesn't surprise me though,' Bill said, in a sober tone. 'Gee, it was easy to fall in love those last two months before D-day. We all knew it was coming you see, and every day that went by we felt closer to combat. Of course the boys fell in love. They fell and they fell hard. I don't blame 'em, either, coz they fell in a hail of bullets that day on the beach. The sea was red with their blood, I'm sorry to have to tell you.'

Tyler was quiet. 'I suppose some of them weren't so lucky, were they?' he said, and his voice was choked with emotion.

'Some of those young fellows never really lived, no,' Bill said. 'I often think of that, because I'm over eighty myself, and I've seen a bit of life passing by. In my mind I'm not like this though, I'm back there with those guys, and we're off duty and we're laughing. We're all listening to the boogie-woogie on the radio. That's how I like to remember them.' There was a pause and then Bill said he was a little tired now.

Emma sighed and sat back in her chair. Tyler went into thanking mode.

'I can't tell you what a privilege it was to have a chance to talk to someone like yourself, sir…'

Bill was just as bad. 'I just want to thank you young people for taking an interest in all this…'

Emma rolled her eyes. With two of them at it, the thank-you speeches could go on forever. They'd be here til dawn running up a gigantic phone bill. Her parents wouldn't be too thrilled about that, even if it had brought them snippets of information.

Susan and Keith didn't look overly concerned about their phone bill, though. They sat side by side on their chintzy couch and held hands. The call had been moving and left them both sad. So many young lives, such a troubled time, such a terrible sacrifice.

Unfortunately, when they all stopped to think about the facts, none of them were really sure if anything concrete had been learned about Joe. They still didn't know his name.

'I wonder if that really was him, the guy who kept running back to help people in the water. I know we can't be sure—it could have been a different man, but it would be nice to think that my grandfather was a hero, of course it would,' Emma said.

Susan was more pragmatic, 'it would also be nice to think that he was a survivor—who lived to tell the tale, dear. I'm not sure that the two are found together, generally speaking.'

Tyler promised that they'd look into it. He knew that the troops had to work their way further into France, capturing various strategic places. They must have had to regroup in various ways. Maybe someone else would know what happened to Joe.

Emma said she was intrigued by the idea of the nickname. 'The men must have liked him and respected him if they went round calling him Chief—Joe was only a private.'

Tyler looked funny when she said that—sort of guilty, like a dog caught with a fluffy slipper. Emma seemed so thrilled by Joe's wartime reputation that he didn't want to say anything more. They were on his trail now. It would all come out soon enough.

# 17

## Bombshell

The results of the DNA test came in the post. The postman walked up the little path to the door of the cottage, pushed the crisp white envelope through the letterbox, and it fluttered down to the ground. It looked so innocuous, lying peacefully on the mat, but it might as well have been a buzz bomb, given the impact it made.

Susan stood it by her teacup while she finished her toast and marmalade. Keith was looking round for his briefcase ready to go to work. Emma poked the letter at her mother. 'Open it, Mum, you spent all that money having it done. Put us all out of our misery.'

Inside was a pamphlet explaining all about DNA testing and margins of error and haplotypes and all sorts of complicated stuff. There were dire warnings about not using the results in support of any racist doctrines or ideas about supremacy.

There was also a nice little certificate with four possible ethnic groups listed on it, and the percentage of each one that the lab had found. Keith said it looked a bit like a score card.

'So what's the verdict, love?' Keith asked, as his wife furrowed her brow.

The results of Susan's DNA test showed that she was 24% Native American and the rest Northern European.

Susan was stunned. *Native American?* She wouldn't have thought that was possible. After a while, she threw back her head and laughed.

'I always thought I was English through and through,' she said, 'I've lived my whole life under that assumption!'

Keith hovered in the doorway, and asked it there was any chance they'd got her test results mixed up with someone else's.

Emma was also very surprised, but it answered a number of questions. People used to look at her dark glossy hair and ask if she was Greek or Italian. She always said no—they were a Devon family, and very English indeed, but now it was all falling into place. Or out of place. This is why Vera was afraid that no one would want to adopt her baby. Vera had described her own baby as 'a funny-looking little thing'. Susan reflected sadly that she had often thought, while she was growing up, that she looked 'wrong'.

'I used to look in the mirror and wonder why my eyes were narrow, or why my hair wasn't more like my mother's, and why my skin tone was curiously sallow. This is the answer, I suppose. Now I know that I'm not *wrong* at all, but I am *different*.'

Emma was struggling to understand the meaning of the percentages, and she glanced down at the mass of information that had been sent with the results. 'Since Vera was European, with blond hair and blue eyes,' Emma began, thoughtfully, 'does that mean that Joe was about 48 per cent Native American? Is that how it works—given that there is a margin for error?'

Keith said that he supposed it meant that Joe, whoever he was, had one 'normal' parent and one Native American parent, a white man and a Native girl maybe, resulting in a person who was 'half and half' as he put it. His word choice was appalling.

Susan practically exploded. 'Keith, I never thought I'd hear my own husband say such things! One 'normal' parent indeed— are you saying his other parent wasn't normal! Of course his parents were both normal. Look at me, I'm completely normal, aren't I?'

'Well, yes dear. Except that you've become a little volatile of late. Really, I was just thinking out loud and didn't have time to put it into better words. I never meant to offend you, love.'

Susan knew perfectly well that her husband—although not a born diplomat—was not really a racist either—just a tactless idiot with an unfortunate turn of phrase. She seethed quietly on the couch. 'Half and half, indeed!' she said. 'That's my father you're talking about, not a carton of semi-skimmed milk!'

\* \* \*

Emma confronted Tyler the minute he came through the door. She told him about the DNA analysis.

'You knew this,' she said. 'You knew all along.'

'I guessed it,' he admitted. 'You've just got that kind of look. More so even than your mom. There's something a little bit exotic about you.'

'Exotic!' Emma said. 'Is that what people call it now? There used to be other names for it, didn't there? —Harsh, ugly names. Mixed blood, half-breed…'

'Don't! No one says those things now.'

Emma sat at the kitchen table, looking at herself in a hand mirror. Every now and again she would lift up the mirror and take another look. It would have been almost funny if it wasn't for her genuine confusion and surprise. Her own face—the face she had seen thousands of times—seemed to tell her a different story today.

'That's why they called him 'Chief' isn't it? It was some kind of racist nickname?'

'I suppose so. I don't think they meant it to be as *pejorative* as it seems today, Emma.'

'What are you talking about?'

'From what I know, those boys volunteered in droves. They wanted a bit of excitement, see the world, like all the other boys, but more than that—they were brought up with the idea of being warriors, you know. They enlisted in big numbers. A lot of them served in the war. So people admired them for their courage and they called them chief, you understand.'

She took another look in the mirror. That look was still there.

'Would you stop worrying about your face. You should be proud,' Tyler told her. Then he smiled and kissed the side of her face. 'Hey, some women would pay good money to get cheekbones like yours.'

Emma couldn't quite believe that a total stranger could look at her and know something so personal about her. Something she didn't even know herself, even though it had been staring her in the face. She felt she had been blind not to see it. Tyler tried to help her.

'Emma, it's understandable that you were kinda confused about who you really are. Here in Devon you probably don't get to hear about that kind of thing all that much. Back home we see people interviewed on TV all the time, talking about these issues. First Americans and all that. It creates an awareness, I suppose.'

'You just looked at me, and you knew.'

'Sort of,' he said, finally. 'I suspected, anyway. The minute Vera said Lakota I knew I was right. It's not just a place. It's a people.'

'My people?' she said, with a measure of astonishment. 'But I'm English.'

'Yes. You are. But you have America in your blood.'

* * *

*May 1944*
Joe knocked at the door of the cottage, his sleek black hair glinting in the sunlight. Vera came out in a summer dress and a combat jacket, a gift from another admirer. Joe had a folded-up blanket under his arm. Vera picked at it, meaningfully.

126

'What's that for, then? You think we're going to get cold on this picnic, Joe?'

'No,' he said, 'I don't think we'll get cold at all.'

'Cheeky.'

He took her arm and led her down the little path, carefully pulling the garden gate closed behind them. They walked down the hill, and then took a turning that led away from the town. They walked for a long time in silence, up along the wooded lane and out towards open country. They passed an old barn and they both looked at it, but they walked on.

'I wondered about that,' Joe said, as they trudged past.

'Too crowded,' Vera said crisply. They walked away up the hill looking for somewhere more agreeable.

Inevitably, Vera's first objective was to eat. The great thing about being posted to a place like this was that she'd had more food in the last three months than in the last three years, or so it sometimes seemed. For a start there were lots of farms around, and that always helped, and then there was all the stuff she got given by the boys. Joe had brought tinned corned beef for the sandwiches, and a can of peaches in syrup. What bliss to taste peaches! She sat looking out across the Devon countryside, feeling content. Their last course had been chocolate, as ever. She could still taste its sweetness in her mouth.

'Would it be too much to ask for a kiss, now?' Joe said, patiently, 'Or do we have to wait a little longer.'

She looked at him. 'You're a nice boy, Joe. And I will miss you when you're gone. I suppose I'll have to give you something.' She put her arms up round his neck, and settled in to enjoy his kiss. Joe's arms went round her too, inside her combat jacket.

'My pretty French doll,' he murmured. He liked the way she looked today. Her fluffy blonde curls, all ruffled by the wind. Baby blue eyes and lots of mascara. And her soft pink mouth—a mouth that looked gentle as long as she didn't open it to speak. Her lips parted now, but only to receive his kiss. He smiled to himself as he lowered her onto the blanket, because as she lay back, her eyes closed.

# 18

## In the Car

They had fallen into the habit of parking up in a quiet lane not far from the air base, since Tyler didn't think it appropriate to take a woman up to his dorm room. The whole thing seemed to make him feel guilty. He looked like he was robbing the Bank of England if he slid a hand up under Emma's shirt to feel the curves of her breasts.

'I guess we could try out the back seat,' he said, with a slight shake in his voice.

'I thought you'd never ask,' she replied cheerfully, and in one agile move she clambered straight over and into the back of the car, brushing against Tyler's shoulder as she went. He was left with a fleeting impression of her slim brown legs, and a single high-heeled shoe, which fell into his lap at the last minute.

'Are you coming?' she enquired, while he hesitated, wondering what to do with her shoe.

'Sure,' he said, and swallowed hard. He tossed her shoe onto the empty passenger seat.

Being taller and more sedate, Tyler exited through the drivers' door and opened the other one, once he'd figured out the lock. He joined her—nervously—on the expanse of black vinyl that could serve as their marriage bed tonight, if he played his cards right.

It was cramped and they couldn't really lie down, but she was warm and eager and pulled him into a series of hasty, fumbling kisses. Tyler could see why this was such a sweet, seductive pleasure. In the dark, he thought how easy it would be to give in, to discard his inhibitions right now, and he could start by taking off her clothes. Her tight little shirt, he could unbutton that, maybe? And he could release her from her black lace bra, if he could find the catch. It was such a pretty, sexy, thing, with its coy little bow in the front. He supposed it was part of a matching set—she'd wear something like that, most likely. He slid his hand up under her skirt to find out. She was warmer and wetter than he had dared to imagine.

But despite the strength of his desire and the overwhelming temptation to strip away the annoying lace impediments and slip inside her, he knew he had to stop. Just when things were really starting to heat up, just when he knew full well that she was ready for what he longed to give, he dragged himself away from her and it was all off. He leapt out of the car and slammed the door. He stood gasping the fresh air, feeling like a fool, or a fish out of water.

They were back in their usual places again. Tyler behind the wheel, Emma sulking in the passenger seat, perplexed and miserable. Clothing rearranged. Normality reinstated. Everything chaste and proper.

Tyler bowed his head, and said he was sorry, really sorry. After a long, long silence he told he that he had been afraid of this moment—scared to even try to be honest with her. She stared straight ahead into the darkness and didn't reply.

'Look, Emma. There's something I need to tell you about my family,' he said, 'and you must listen and try to understand, because it has a bearing on you and me.'

'What?'

There was a long pause. He put his arm on the steering wheel. 'It's difficult…'

'Come on Tyler, what is it? Or do you want me to guess? You're directly descended from General Custer?'

'No. Not as far as I know.'

'You aren't actually human at all, which is why we can't have sex?'

He smiled at that, and looked away, out towards the darkened sea. 'Emma, my parents have some quite strong views on certain things. They're kinda religious, and some would say they have a moral code which is different to a lot of people.'

'Oh no. They're not like those people who live in the desert, are they? You know, one guy, five wives and twenty-eight children?'

'No! We're just a regular family: my mom and dad, and me and my little brother. Look, they're really good people. They always taught me that even if the rest of the world is doin' it, it don't make it right, y'know? I respect them a lot for what they are trying to do. I know they *strongly* disapprove of any… activity… that doesn't occur within the confines of marriage.'

'The *confines* of marriage! That sound's terrible!' She laughed, but he looked perfectly serious. She began to worry about where this was going. 'But Tyler, you don't go along with all of that, do you?'

'To some extent, I do. I like to think I've been brought up right.'

'To what extent?' she said, in dismay. 'You said you had girlfriends, back home.'

'Yeah. I did, and I am ashamed to say that I have done some things my parents wouldn't be too proud of. And since I met you, it's getting harder and harder to keep their ideals in my mind.'

Emma sighed. She really didn't want their ideals in her mind either. She wanted another kiss, another touch, another taste. She wanted Tyler. She tried to reach out for him, but he shook his head.

'I really like you, Emma, but you have got to understand where I'm comin' from. Look, all I want to do is wait until the time is right. Until we're both sure, you know. Sometimes I think the only reason you like me is because I'm American and you've got some idea in your head about finding out what it was like for your grandmother!'

'That isn't how I feel at all! I don't know how you can say that! I had no idea about the American connection when we met, Tyler, you KNOW that. You must be able to see—'

'Why can't *you* see?' he said, with the first hint of anger she'd ever heard in his voice, 'I am a man with principles, Emma, I can't just toss them away like yesterday's newspaper. It's important to me! You're asking me to forget everything that matters just to play fast and loose with you!'

She looked at him sharply. 'Is that what you think I am,' she said, in anger and disbelief, 'FAST and LOOSE!' She turned away and bit her lip.

'Well, you are a bit...' he began.

'Tyler! For heaven's sake. I'm young and I'm in love and I wanted to share it all with you—to *give* myself to you—and you're too busy thinking about your bloody principles to see how lucky you are!'

'I had a feeling I'd mess this up, Emma. But I know I'm lucky, I do. Please try to understand.'

She stared at the dashboard, blinking back tears. It would be humiliating to let him see how much this had upset her. It did not escape her attention that although he said he was *lucky*, he didn't say he was *in love*. She should not have spoken. He must be right. She was a fast woman with a loose tongue. Or an over-keen, gushy girl with naïve hopes? Either way it was embarrassing. She tried not to say anything more.

They drove to the base. She glanced up at him once or twice while he was concentrating on the driving. He had a handsome face, good in profile. She could well believe he didn't have any trouble finding girlfriends, but she began to wonder how good he was at keeping them. She began to think about how much longer his deployment in the UK would last, and who would fix her broken heart after he'd gone.

When they reached the gates of the airbase, Emma reminded him that her parents were out on Friday night so they'd have the place to themselves. He said he had to work.

'But you said you were free that night.' She got out of the car to go round to the driver's side.

'I was, but I swapped shifts.'

'Did they ask you to do that?' she said sharply.

'No, I... erm... sort of... requested it.'

'You *asked* to work Friday night, so that *you wouldn't have to be alone with me!*'

She looked very, very hurt. She flounced into the car, slammed the door, and put the car in gear to go.

'Emma!' he called out. 'Emma! I can explain. It's not that I don't want to spend time with you!'

He wanted to tell her that back home, the pastor used to advise that sometimes we have the opportunity and sometimes we have the inclination, and the key to staying on the narrow path is never to let the two come together. He was only doing what he thought was right.

It was too late. Emma was already performing an angry three-point turn, stabbing the car in and out of gear. She was crying. He could see that she was in no mood to listen to his ideas about the opportunity and the inclination. He sure hoped she'd calm down and drive carefully.

The man on sentry duty at the barrier made a face at Tyler. 'Lovers' tiff, is it? What have you done wrong now, young fella?'

Tyler ignored him, and trudged along the concrete path towards the base. He hadn't gone more than a hundred yards when he got a text message. From Emma.

'I don't think it's going to work out,' it said, and he stared at the screen in alarm. She must have pulled over on the road just outside the base to send this. She was upset. Very, very upset. He'd run after her if only he had time, but he was late already and right now he had to get changed and report for duty. He sent straight back, to try to calm her down.

'Don't be hasty, baby,' he wrote. He pressed send. He hoped it would help.

The reply came stinging back almost instantly. She was lightening fast at this.

'Not much chance of that with you, is there?'

That one scared him. He frowned at the phone. He decided not to send another message in case it made things worse. He had to go inside and get changed. He had work to do.

* * *

Helen came straight over, for a council of war, when she heard how upset Emma was. Her advice was plain and easy to follow. It was also completely unpalatable.

'Face it, Emma. He isn't interested. He's a time-waster. Cut your losses. Move on. '

'But I don't want to move on. I like him, I love being with him, I just want more of him, that's all.'

'Emma. Has it occurred to you that maybe he changed his shift because he's got a date with someone else? Maybe he's got another girlfriend and he's phasing you out, and phasing her in. Some guys do that so they don't have any gaps in between. Maybe it's over. Finished.'

'How can it be finished when it hasn't really begun?'

'If it hasn't begun, why is it so hard to disentangle yourself. I thought you said you'd learnt from the whole thing with Matthew and this time you weren't going to fall so far and so fast.'

'I have, though, there was nothing I could do.'

'I can't think why—Tyler's not exactly a laugh a minute, except by accident. The longest conversation I've ever had with him was about a potato!' Helen said. 'Emma, he's a bit of a rebound guy, isn't he? That's probably why you ended up with someone 'safe', someone who doesn't even want—'

'He does want to,' she protested, 'I'm sure he wants to, he's just holding back for some stupid reason and I don't know why! Oh Helen, when he kisses me, it's so—'

'Spare me! I'd rather talk about interest rates or tax returns. Listen to me, Emma. I don't want you to make a fool of yourself, that's all. Do not, under any circumstances phone him up and beg him to talk. If there is to be any hope for you and this man it has to come from him. You can never make a person like you more by begging them to. Do you understand? You promise. Wait for him to make the next move. If there isn't a move, then come out with me Saturday night and we'll set up a new audition for the role of Mr Right, because I have a horrible suspicion that it isn't Mr Robinson.'

Emma thought she could count on kind words from her parents —she was sure they liked Tyler. She was stunned when they said they wouldn't be sorry if it was over.

'Can't you see,' Keith said, 'your mother and I don't like the idea of you getting serious with a young man in the forces. We don't want you trailing around from place to place following the military. He'll get sent to awful places. Trouble spots. And you might be sitting around waiting for him—waiting for news, waiting to hear if he's alive or dead. Imagine that, Emma—and what if you had his kiddies, love?'

Emma's face looked stricken. She had never even dared to look that far ahead. Susan touched her daughter's hand. 'I think perhaps we'd all heave a sigh of relief if things didn't go any further with Tyler. We've nothing against him, of course. He's lovely. But we'd rather you found someone else. We hope you understand. Oh, sweetie, I'm sorry. I know you really liked him.'

* * *

Tyler stood outside the chapel reading the notice board. There was just one small building that all the denominations used. There was quite a tight roster, even during the week. It was amazing how many people needed some kind of spirituality when they were in the security forces. They do say there never was an atheist in a foxhole. He looked closely at the timetable, wondering when he could get a bit of pastoral care, a bit of fatherly advice, even. Not for a while, by the look of it. The Jewish guys were in there at the moment. After that the Catholic contingent got their turn, and there were plenty of them. His lot didn't get a look in until tomorrow morning. Maybe the chaplain wasn't the guy to see about this anyway. He could always try Bradley, instead.

'I'll give you a piece of advice, if you want it.' Bradley said, banging his locker door shut. *'Forget her.* That girl is getting too clingy, Tyler. There is something else you could do first though, if you want to, and it also begins with 'F'. Try it. Get her out of your system. Then forget about her. Works every time. You'll have to turn your phone off for a while, though, afterwards. That's what I always do.'

Tyler knew what his parents would say if he tried to speak to them. For a start they'd be alarmed if he broke the established pattern and phoned them at an irregular time. He phoned them every week, at exactly eight pm on a Tuesday night, without fail. In between he sent brief emails telling them work was good and the weather was not. They wrote back with all the small town news about who had a new tractor and what the mayor was up to (which was never all that exciting). It would startle them if he phoned on a Thursday. It would startle them even more if he tried to talk about Emma, and how he felt about her.

* * *

*May 1944*
Joe's company got moved to a new campsite, only half a mile from the bay. They called it 'the marshalling area'. It was a strong sign that the order to invade France was close, very close. Vera noticed more and more activity in the harbour too. She bor-

rowed a pair of binoculars and tried to make out what was going on. People scurrying about, large heavy objects draped in netting, stuff disappearing into the holds of the ships, and a row of armoured cars driven right through the town and onto the fisherman's wharf.

Strict controls were placed on people entering or leaving the area. People who wandered in by mistake had to stay. It all added to the mounting sense that something was about to happen. With all that cloak and dagger stuff going on in the harbour, Vera didn't expect to be invited into the dragon's lair. But she was. Joe told her a dance was to be held at the camp. He'd like her to come. He was afraid it might be the last one for a while.

'It won't be the last dance, Joe. But if your lot gets the word and has to go, it'll be the last one that you get to go to.'

'You got such a way with words, baby doll.'

'I'm a realist, that's all.'

'Will you be alright, Vera, while I'm in France?'

'Course I will, Joe. For a start I ain't gonna be lonely. I'm sure your old camp site is filling up with a new lot, even as we speak.'

'That does worry me, a little.'

'Well, don't. I told you. I can take care of myself.'

'Yeah, I know, but I'd like to be here to do it for you, that's all.'

'I would have liked that too, Joe. Now get out of here before I start snivelling.'

That day, while she was working in the canteen a number of other young men invited her too. Each time another young fellow started beating around the bush about the dance, she told him straight that she knew all about the do at the army camp, thanks. Halfway through her shift, Vera's supervisor called the girls together and said that transport would be provided for them if they'd like to go to the dance at the camp.

Vera experienced a rare moment of surprise. 'It must be bad, if starchy old Mrs Whatsit wants us to go. They must know the boys are going soon.'

Miranda had grown up a fair bit since she arrived at the canteen, but she was a little shocked all the same. 'This whole idea of *trucking in the wenches* does seem a little debauched, doesn't it?'

'Well, you wouldn't want to die without knowing what love was like, would you, dear?' The comment came from starchy Mrs Whatsit, whose husband's name was on the monument in the high street. At forty-five she didn't consider herself old or starchy. She too was planning to attend the dance at the camp that night.

# 19

## The Ancestors

On Friday night, Emma tried to take her mind off Tyler by doing a lot of Internet research. She stayed up for hours looking at different websites about 'First Americans' and rights and issues. One piece of information kept leading to another and another, until finally she found an expert on the history of the Lakota. The potted biography of him said that he lived on a reservation, and was a great authority on all things Native American.

The exciting thing was that he was online and ready to talk to her. They could have a conversation in real time, and he could explain a number of things about 'her heritage'. They could have the interview right now, if she wanted.

She did. She was nervous but she wanted to know a little more. His image came over the web cam and into the room.

'Hi Emma, nice to meet you! I'm Charlie. Can you see me alright?'

She could, but he wasn't what she was expecting. Charlie was a large man, dressed in an old grey sweatshirt. The shirt had some kind of baseball team slogan on the front. He had a two skinny pigtails coming down on either side of his wide neck. He didn't look like any kind of historian Emma had ever encountered before, but she was prepared to put her scepticism aside and listen to what he had to say.

There was something about the plain, gentle way he spoke about the Lakota that won her respect. Also, he had a look about him that reminded her of her own mother. It would be too much to claim *a family resemblance*, of course, but there was just something about the weather beaten face and the eyes.

Charlie explained that Dakota and Lakota are two strands of the same Sioux people—the meaning of the word is the same.

'What does it mean?' Emma asked him. 'I know nothing of the language.'

'It means 'friends' or 'allies',' he told her.

Emma felt a stab of emotion at that word. The Allies. That's what Joe was. He was one of the Allies. He had come over here to help them out, and all he wanted was to find a bit of adventure along the way. To live a little, to meet people and see some places. Heaven only knew what had happened to Joe in the end. She forgot about the web cam and let the tears come. She put both hands up to wipe them away.

'Take some time and come back to this,' Charlie told her, and there was a lot of compassion in his voice. 'You will have many questions. You can come and talk to me again.' He recommended some more web sites where she could learn a little about her ancestors. 'I have to warn you, Emma, history isn't pretty.'

On her own she looked at the images. She saw tribal people dancing to unfamiliar music and singing in their native language. She saw young people talking about their land and their customs. She heard about those who died for those things, too.

Other things came as a surprise too. For the first time she saw images of young women like herself—with long dark hair and high cheekbones—represented as beautiful, truly beautiful.

Emma spent a long time just looking in the mirror and trying to get used to the idea. She even braided her hair just to see what it would look like. Embarrassed, she pulled it all free again. She decided that her face did indeed carry the echoes of her ancestors. She was a living reminder of people who inhabited another world—a frightening world that she knew nothing about. The Sioux say that a people with no history is like the wind over the buffalo grass. She went back to her computer and read some more. Tribesmen on the plains, arrows, knives, and tomahawks. It was a far cry from what she was used to. Emma's world was the soft green countryside and the wandering hedgerows. It was a picturesque place bathed in pale English sunlight. It was the cottage she called home, with the roses round the door. At first Emma could only see the differences, until she found that the Lakota say that 'we are all related.' The Dakota have another saying, and it made her think of Joe: 'we will be known forever by the tracks we leave.'

\* \* \*

Tyler looked at the digital clock on the wall, willing it to signal the end of the night's work. The minute his shift ended at one a.m. he was out of there. He had to see her. He washed the oil off his hands but he didn't stop to change out of his overalls or his steel-capped boots. There were no buses at that time of night. He walked for quite a few miles hoping to hitch a lift. Quite a few cars drove past, but he got no offers. He supposed they were nervous about picking up a stranger at this time of night. He prayed that he didn't have to walk the whole way—it would take forever.

\* \* \*

**May 1944**

The dance hall was alive with people. The music was loud and ridiculously cheerful. The atmosphere was all forced merriment and desperate gaiety. Young women in civilian dress peppered the dance floor—every one of them in the arms of a man in uniform. All the girls had tried so hard to be glamorous, cheering up a shabby summer frock with an artificial flower or a borrowed cardigan. Their hairstyles were just like the stars of stage and screen, and their lips were painted bright scarlet—it made them look quite gaudy.

Joe had to keep on dancing with Vera—if they stopped for a break another soldier would ask her to dance with him instead. They didn't hold back. Not tonight. Joe didn't want his girl to take up a better offer.

He began to get impatient. 'Do you want to go get some fresh air, Vera, it's kinda crowded in here, isn't it?'

'No it isn't, and it's getting less and less crowded all the time. I reckon there are more couples out there in the dark than there are in here on the dance floor.'

'Come on, Vera, you can't tell me that you don't like to tango.'

'They're playing a quickstep, Joe.' She seemed resolutely determined to misunderstand him.

'I know,' he said. 'But I sure would like to tango.'

'I'll bet you would, Joe, but I don't know. Out there, with all that lot? There's no privacy.'

He led her by the hand to where the blackout curtains covered the doorway. 'Come on, girl. We're different; we're not like the rest. We're in love. We won't even notice the other people. It'll just be you and me, in the dark.'

Vera's pretty face looked tired and cynical just the same. 'What on earth do you think is different about that!'

* * *

Tyler was beginning to think he'd been mad to try to hitch a lift to Emma's place. Then, finally, a guy in a delivery van gave him a lift and took him the rest of the way. He dropped him off outside the door of the cottage in the early hours. It had taken over three hours to get there.

There were faint signs of the early morning light. Tyler knew it was not a polite time to call, but he wasn't giving up now. He sent her a text: 'I'm outside your house, I have to see you.' He pressed send and hoped she'd get it.

She appeared at the upstairs window and looked down at him in surprise.

'What do you want?'

He couldn't think of anything smart to say, but he looked up at her like he was a stray dog that needed to be taken in.

She came downstairs and opened the door. She was in her nightdress. He pulled her into a long, aching kiss in the doorway.

A lorry rattled past quite close, and the driver hooted at them, but they didn't even notice. This road, the one outside her house, was the same road the troops and their vehicles travelled as they made their way to the coast for the invasion. It was as if they passed by now, a rumbling procession of trucks and jeeps and men. A ghost train long since gone.

'Do you think he even got the chance to say goodbye?' Tyler asked her. 'That day when they had to go to Normandy?'

'I don't know. Maybe not—I think they sealed the camps for about a while before they left. Tyler, is that why you're here?' she asked, 'to say good bye.'

'No. No, Emma. I don't want to say goodbye. There's no reason for us to say goodbye.' He held her and kissed her again. 'May we go upstairs, now? We could talk there?'

'If you want to.'

'I really want to.'

They went up the tiny creaking cottage stairs and into Emma's room. Her laptop was still playing the Native American images as a screen saver.

'You've found some stuff on the Lakota?' he said.

'Yes. Their story breaks my heart. It's hard to read.'

'I know.'

'I have to read it, though. I want to know, because it's part of me,' she said. She shivered. 'Did you know about what happened at Wounded Knee? And what the soldiers did there? To the women and the children?'

'I know what they did,' Tyler admitted.

'It's a lot to take in, all at once. Quite a shock. I can show you some of the websites, if you want?'

'Yes, I'd like that, but not now.'

He took a step towards her. The room was tiny, and she was right there, but he felt like he was crossing the Mississippi river. She must have sensed the significance of the moment.

'What is it, Tyler? What do you want?'

'You know what I want, Emma. I want you so bad—I never wanted anything as much as I want you.'

She hesitated. 'Are you sure it's me you want? Or is it just because you like the idea of someone exotic?'

'I can't pretend I didn't notice that. It drew me to you. But you are *you*. The one I love. The woman I want for myself.' He reached out to touch her. 'And if you come here, I'll show you how much I love you.'

It was ironic, he thought. Now that he wanted to, she was shying away like a wild pony. He had to coax her, stroke her, and reassure her. He didn't even try to take her clothes off for a while. They just kissed until she was ready to trust him. There was no need to hurry.

'I shouldn't have got so upset, should I?' she said. 'I could have been more understanding. I've always thought that if you care about someone, you should to try to respect their views, and I *do* care about you, Tyler, really I—'

'Shush,' he said. 'I know you love me. I think you fell a little in love with me that night you took my hand, isn't that right?'

She nodded, 'but I have fallen a lot further since then.'

'So have I.'

'But, Tyler, what if things change? What if we get torn apart?'

'If we are ever parted, aren't we gonna wish we'd had every minute we could have together?'

She couldn't argue with that.

She seemed to understand that he meant business when he took off his boots and his coverall—she called it a 'boiler suit'. She said he could leave it on the chair. She lay quietly on the bed and waited for him, but he didn't make her wait too long. Not this time. He hauled his t-shirt off over his head.

'What about—' she began.

'I've got some,' he said. 'They're in my pocket.'

She looked surprised. 'So you have actually thought about this, then?'

'Honey, I've been thinking about it night and day since we met.'

He was amazed by his own determination to carry out this dawn raid upon her. He thought he'd feel shy with her, but he didn't. What a luxury it was, to touch her and taste her and not even think about when to stop. To caress the warm contours of her breasts, to seek out the moist secrets of her body, and to hear her sighing just for him. He knew that she had been longing for this, aching for his touch, her whole body begging him to love her, and right now it seemed crazy that he had ever held back. At last, he could enjoy her and give her everything she wanted.

So they were joined together, as man has joined with woman since the beginning. There was something almost primitive and almost sacred about it. As he took her, he looked down and saw a glint of proud passion in those dark eyes of hers. He felt the sweet surrender of her body as he moved inside her. He thrust harder and higher until he knew that the only thing that mattered was this urgent struggle to possess her, and in the last driving push to meet his own need and hers, he truly believed that they would be joined for all time. He lost himself completely in her arms, and he did not want to be found.

Too soon, it ebbed away; leaving him with the regretful understanding that this was, indeed, only a moment's pleasure.

Afterwards they lay together and he stroked her hair for a long time. It was a peaceful, blissful moment, and Emma felt content. She nuzzled against him and he kissed her forehead.

'You know,' he said. 'That was my first time.'

Emma almost laughed. 'Tyler, don't ruin it. I know you're only joking.'

'No,' he said. 'I'm not.'

She turned to look at him and she could he was telling the truth. Her eyes widened. He was looking straight back at her with the puppy dog expression again. No dimples. Just serious eyes and heartfelt sincerity. She was surprised she hadn't realised. It explained a lot, really. Not many guys stop to read the instructions on the packet first. She had thought it was all part of his got-to-be-done-properly mentality.

'I couldn't lose you, just because I was afraid to love you,' he said. 'After I got that worked out, the decision was easy.'

She melted and gave him a kiss. 'Oh, Tyler,' she said and stroked his face, 'I hope it was ok, in that case.' Emma knew she could be reasonably confident on that score, but she understood that it was an emotional experience as well as a physical one.

'It was sensational,' he said.

Emma's father opened the door to tell her it was eight o'clock.

'Pardon me!' he said, and closed the door very quickly.

Tyler was mortified with embarrassment. 'I thought you said your parents were *out for the night*,' he said, sitting up in bed. A flush of shame radiated out across his face and neck, spreading down onto his chest.

'They only went out for dinner. They got back just after nine. Did you think I meant something else?'

Clearly, he had. These little slips between meaning and understanding were always happening to them, since they each spoke a dialect, in effect.

'Sorry,' she said, 'American English and English English are not as similar as you might think.'

'Emma, this is awful. Your dad will think I have no respect for you!'

'No he won't, Tyler. He likes you—he does. He told me—'

'Listen!'

There were voices just outside the bedroom door again. Emma's mum was on the landing and Emma's dad was calling out to tell her not to go in.

'She'll want her cup of tea, Keith, she always wants her cup of tea,' Susan insisted.

The handle on the door moved, and Tyler sort of clutched at the duvet as if he might try to dive underneath it.

Keith's voice was heard again. 'Don't go in, Susie,' he called out. 'She's got the American boy in there!'

'Oh, *I see*! I'll leave her to it, then.'

There was a pause, and then a cautious knock on the door. Susan called out that she was going downstairs to cook the breakfast and there would be plenty for everyone.

'OK, thanks mum!' Emma said, as if this happened every weekend. She turned to Tyler, who looked very, very uncomfortable.

'Are you staying for breakfast?' she said, 'I should think its bacon and eggs, as it's a Saturday.'

Susan Rowland cooked as if she was feeding the troops. The full English breakfast: bacon and eggs, sizzling tomatoes and plenty of rounds of hot buttered toast. The Rowlands liked to have enough time for a leisurely breakfast before Emma went off to teach the swim squad.

After a bit of a pep talk from Emma, Tyler was persuaded to come downstairs and eat with them. He only agreed because the smell of the fried bacon was completely intoxicating, and he hadn't eaten anything since before his shift yesterday. It had all been so hectic since the arrival of the results of the DNA test.

Keith tried to put the young man at his ease by making some hot coffee, which was gratefully accepted, but Tyler still couldn't look him in the eye.

It was quite comical really. Mr and Mrs Rowland made conversation about the weather and the upcoming swimming competition. Emma ran round looking for the bottom half of her black bikini, and Tyler sat with his head down, trying to eat his breakfast as if he was invisible.

'Finished that lot, lad? You seem to have quite an appetite! Are you up for second helpings?' The words were out before

Keith could stop them. Tyler's face was a sight to see. A martyred look of mortification with a beetroot red blush.

Susan busied herself at the sink so that she could suppress her giggles.

Tyler looked nervously at the kitchen clock. He said he hadn't realized how late it was and he supposed he should get back to the base. He had another shift starting in a few hours, and he hadn't gotten any sleep.

'No, I don't suppose you've had the chance.' Keith said, with a glance at Emma, and a wink.

Susan told her husband not to tease. 'You must get some sleep, Tyler. It would be very irresponsible to go to work on something as important as an aeroplane without any sleep. Mistakes might happen.'

'Borrow my car and go straight there,' Emma said, and tossed him the keys, 'Dad will take me to the swimming pool, won't you?'

Tyler made ready to leave, issuing the customary thank-you speeches to Emma's parents before heading for the door. The excellence of the coffee... the lovely breakfast... no better way to start to the day (bit more of a blush, just there). Apologies for the hasty departure... better run.

Emma looked up. 'Don't I get a kiss?'

He gave her a chaste peck on the cheek, and fled. She sighed. It was back to all that again.

When he had gone Susan and Keith were convulsed with laughter. Susan had to grab a tea towel and wipe tears of laughter from the corners of her eyes.

'You finally talked him into it, then, you little minx!' Keith observed.

'That sweet boy, away from home and missing his family, he didn't stand a chance, did he?' Susan smiled at her daughter.

'Probably about time he took the plunge,' Keith said, and laughed.

'Is the whole story that obvious?' Emma said, with wide-eyed surprise. Honestly, her parents were beyond belief.

'Yes, I'm afraid it is.' Susan looked out of the window at her tiny English garden and sighed. 'Ah well, that's what makes the world go round, isn't it? Just remember though, he's only in England for a while. Don't get too fond of him, will you? I don't want him to break your heart, like Joe broke Vera's.'

She turned to Emma. 'I don't suppose you've heard any more about what happened on D-Day, have you?'

# 20

## A Kiss and a Promise

Bill, the veteran from Maryland, sent Emma a letter and said there was very little else he could tell, but he'd found a photo of a few of the guys just before they left the south coast. Two of them were medics who went with the guys to Normandy. His mate Joe was on the right. He hoped it was the Joe they were looking for.

Emma could hardly believe she was holding a photograph of the man who might, just might, have been her grandfather. She stared at the man on the right. She stared and stared, and tried to take it in. He looked normal enough, standing there in his army uniform: orderly dress, they called it, complete with a collar and tie. *What on earth was I expecting?* She asked herself. *Feathers?*

He looked a bit like the young Gregory Peck. Tall, with dark hair, neatly cut. Eyes narrowed against the sun—or maybe they were just like that. Handsome. Someone you might fall for. Someone Vera might have fallen for.

Emma sat looking at her reflection for a long time, and thought about her own looks. She'd got the dark hair, something about the eyes, and the high cheekbones. She compared it with the photo. It could easily have been him, she thought. She went to show it to her mother.

\* \* \*

Tyler came to see her every night that week; there was no stopping him now. On Thursday he brought his washing with him, which Keith said was a bit of a cheek. On Friday, he turned up at the cottage door with a big cardboard box in his arms.

'What's all this?' Susan asked, when she opened the front door. 'Emma's still at school, you know, for the swimming competition.'

'I know. I hope they win. I got you a few things, at the shop at the base.' Tyler came through to the kitchen to unpack it.

'Heavens, you didn't need to bring us all this!' Susan started going through the items and putting them in the cupboards.

'Well I'm here such a lot now, and I didn't want to eat you out of house and home.'

Susan smiled at him, 'you are very welcome here, Tyler.' Then she turned away to hide the grimace that crossed her face when she saw the American beer.

'Thank you,' he said, he stared at twee little birdhouse in the middle of the lawn. The cat was circling it, rubbing its tail on the wooden post. 'Thank you for saying that, Mrs Rowland, I appreciate every bit of your hospitality. I just want you to know that I really care about Emma. She means the world to me.'

'Baloney,' Susan said, and Tyler looked at her in alarm. She was reading from the label on one of the packets of food. 'Is it nice?' she asked, innocently.

'Yes, very nice. A lot of people really like it. Anyway, Mrs Rowland, I was telling you about my feelings for Emma—'

'Yes. You were.'

'I've told her that I love her.'

'I'm sure you have, dear. They all do. Matthew used to say it a lot.'

'Matthew—that's the guy she used to know in—'

'That awful man in Manchester, yes.' Susan inspected an enormous packet of pork spare ribs, in sticky brown sauce. 'What do I do with these?'

'You put 'em on the grill. Do you have a grill outside?' he looked doubtfully in the direction of the tiny garden.

'Do you mean a barbecue? No. Could we cook them in here, do you think? Or would they create a lot of smoke?'

'I'm sure we could sort something out. I can't cook 'em at the base, you see, I've only got a microwave and a hotplate.' He gazed lustfully at the spare ribs. 'They are absolutely great with fried potatoes. Or mashed potatoes. Or any kind of potatoes.'

Tyler had that doggie-wants-a-bone-look again. Susan was tempted to ruffle his hair.

'Shall I try to cook them tonight, for you, then?'

'Would you?'

'Yes. Emma is always fretting about what we should feed you.'

'She's wonderful. I mean it when I say...'

'Don't, Tyler. It's bad enough watching it all unfold, without all the false assurances that go with it. She came back from Manchester a complete mess. She adored Matthew. Keith and I were hoping she'd forget about men for a while. We tried to encourage her to concentrate on her career and enjoy life. But no, she has to go and meet you.'

'I'm different, Mrs Rowland.'

Susan didn't want to listen anymore; she was reaching into the bottom of the cardboard box.

'Ooh, chocolates! And they look delicious, too. Not exactly healthy heart food, but I don't suppose we'll be able to resist!'

Tyler smiled. He was hoping the chocolates would soften her up. Then he heard Emma call out as she came through the front door and he ran to meet her and give her a kiss. 'Hey baby, did they win?'

'No, but we got silver! The girls were thrilled.' Emma looked pretty pleased about it herself.

'That's fantastic,' he said, with real admiration.

'Yes it is, and we were also awarded Most Improved Team, because we came nineteenth out of twenty last year.'

Tyler pulled her close and spoke low, so her mother wouldn't hear. 'I'm surprised you didn't bring home Sexiest Swim Coach too,' he whispered, brimful of happiness.

'I never thought I'd hear you say something like that!' she said.

* * *

### June 1st 1944

Joe raced along the street to meet Vera at the monument. They couldn't meet on the pier anymore; it was blocked off ready for loading the troops onto the boats. He knew he was on his last pass out of the camp. A guy in the cookhouse knew someone who typed out memos of importance, and the word was that from tomorrow, all leave would be cancelled. He ran all the way, not wanting to waste a single minute. All he wanted was time that he could spend with her. Up ahead, he saw her waiting for him, by the monument. He hoped she would be pleased to see him.

She was standing there with her arms folded, and her back to him, reading the names of those who fell in the Great War.

'Hey, baby!' he said, and arrived beside her. He hadn't seen her for five days. They'd taken the guys from his company on a training exercise up in the hills. They'd used live ammunition and a number of men had been hurt. It had been Joe's first glimpse of any type of combat, and although it was staged and planned, it scared the hell out of him. If people got hurt when everyone was trying *not* to shoot each other, he hated to think what it would be like when they faced the enemy.

Vera just collapsed against him, and cried her eyes out. 'I thought you were gone already,' she told him, 'I thought I'd seen the last of you.'

She wasn't usually like this—shaky and vulnerable.

'You alright, Vera?'

She told him what she thought had happened…

'No! Really?' he said. 'Are you sure?'

'I reckon I am, Joe, I've never been this late before.'

She kept pacing up and down beside the monument, smoking her cigarette, with her other arm folded across her body in a gesture of self-protection. She looked as skinny as anything, but he knew Vera didn't joke about stuff like this.

A broad, slow, smile spread itself across Joe's face.

She looked up at him, and this time—as she passed by—she slapped him.

'Ouch! What did you have to do that for?'

'Because you look like you just scored for England, that's why! What about me, Joe? What's going to happen to me? When my landlady finds out, I'll lose my lodgings, and I can't even get back to London now they've sealed the area. Bloody hell, Joe, I swore I'd never let this happen to me. I promised my ma I wouldn't get caught out.'

'I'll take care of you.'

'No you won't Joe. Of course you won't. You'll be over there, taking care of everyone else. The orders will come anytime now. They're sure to want to make use of this fine weather. If Jerry doesn't get you, them French girls will. I shall have to take care myself, like I always do.'

'I'm coming back. I'll write and tell you when.'

'I'm not sitting around waiting for letters that don't come.'

'I'll write as soon as I can, Vera. I won't let you down.'

'That's what they all say.'

'I'm not like the rest,'

'Yes you are. Exactly like the rest. Are you telling me there wasn't someone back home you said goodbye to? Is she waiting for a letter an all?'

He didn't say yes, and he didn't say no, but he knew he wore a guilty face.

'I'll have to get myself back to London and get it taken care of,' Vera said, and she shook her head as if she couldn't quite believe it all herself.

That scared Joe a lot—that phrase—*get it taken care of.*

'When you say that, Vera, I hope you don't mean—' There was a catch in his voice, but he swallowed and tried again. He knew he had to try to persuade her. He'd have to leave her soon, and there were no guarantees. This was his last hope, his last try. 'Look, baby, don't you see, if anything happens to me, I'd like to think I'd left someone to follow in my footsteps—that little one I've given you—that might be my only son.'

'Or your *daughter*, Joe, and what kind of life can I give her?'

'Vera. I want you to tell me the truth. If I didn't come back, for any reason, you wouldn't do anything hasty, would you?

'I don't want to make you no promises. We are in no situation to be making each other promises.'

He told her it was his last pass. He told her that if there ever was a day to make each other a promise, it was today, because there wouldn't be another chance for a long, long time.

'Oh you poor boy,' she said, and she cupped his face in her hands. 'I'm not saying I'll keep it, but I'll make you a promise if that's what you want. What is it you want me to say?'

'I want you to make them all, of course.'

'I don't understand, Joe.'

'All the promises, baby doll. I want to hear you say 'em. I want you to tell me you'll wait for me. And that you'll always love me, and you'll have our kid, and she'll grow up in a better world, and when the war is over, everything will be all right. I want all that, today. Promise me. I need you to do that for me today.'

So Vera sat down on the cold stone steps that led up to the monument to the fallen. Some would say she was one of them now—a fallen woman. She sat with her Joe, and she made every promise he wanted her to make. She told him everything she thought he'd want to hear, and they kissed and they cried and they held onto each other's hands.

After a while, they got up to go. They wanted to find somewhere a bit more cheerful to spend their last little bit of together. Vera looked back at the monument. 'Don't go being a hero, you hear? I don't want to see your name on one of these, etched on a cold bit of marble. Not your name, Joe, because that should be mine. I want your name for myself.'

# 21

## Ready or Not

Saturday morning, Tyler was lying in Emma's bed, trying to ignore the sunlight filtering in through the curtains. He loved waking up with her and wrapping his arms around her. Sometimes she let him make love to her again in the mornings, if there was time. He traced his fingers across her back and down her shoulder blade, admiring the warm copper sheen on her skin. But she didn't turn to face him. Not today. She was reading a book—reading about the day that the orders came to leave.

'According to this, the month of May was hot and sunny in 1944,' Emma said, 'but on June 1$^{st}$ the weather broke, and it was bad for days. The men were cooped up in the ships ready to leave, and the planes were standing by—they were planning to drop a lot of guys with parachutes too. The fields were full of tanks and howitzers, too, lined up and waiting for the word go.'

'Yeah, everything was ready for action,' Tyler said, and he leant across to look at the book too, kissing her shoulder on the way. She didn't seem to mind. He whispered low in her ear. 'So am I, sweetheart.'

She smiled but she ignored him. 'It says here that the only thing that didn't come to the party was the weather. The Generals got panicky and held a meeting about it, but they made the decision to go ahead. Eisenhower wrote a note taking full responsibility in case it all went wrong, and he tucked it away in case he needed it. Then he gave the order to leave.'

He didn't answer, he was kissing her neck. But Emma was too preoccupied. She got out of bed and swathed herself in her pink satin gown, an action that Tyler found rather frustrating. He tried to pull her back. 'Hey! Where are you going, baby?'

'I want to check my email,' she said. 'I'm expecting another message from the veterans' association.' She sat down at her little desk, and checked her messages.

Tyler smiled to think she'd rather do that than the activity he had in mind.

'Here it is! The message. It says here that there *is* a survivor from the group that medic was with. The one you think is Joe.'

'That's great, sweetie. What else does it say?'

'It says that we should talk to him if we want to know more; apparently he's very old and very deaf. It says he's in our part of the world right now, so we should grab the chance and get in touch.'

'Does he live nearby?'

'No, but he's not in the States either, he's just taken a flight to Normandy for the Anniversary of D-Day, which is being 'celebrated'—if that's the right word—next week. He's with a whole group of other World War Two Vets.'

'So they are in France? Right now? Just across the way?' Tyler said, sitting up in bed.

'Yes.'

Tyler looked at her and she looked at him.

'I don't suppose there's any way we could—' Emma hesitated. She was afraid to say it. She knew it wouldn't be possible. She knew the flights would most likely be full, and the trains, and even if they got tickets, it would be difficult to get time off work at short notice, and probably Tyler would need to apply in triplicate three months ahead with the Department of Defence. But it was too tantalising, the thought of actually being able to talk to someone who knew Joe.

Emma sat down on the bed and braced herself for the disappointment. Tyler would be really sweet about it—she knew that—but he wouldn't go tearing off to France at a moment's notice. He did not believe in acting in haste. He leant towards her and took her hand.

'This means a lot to you, doesn't it, baby?'

'Yes.'

'What was it Eisenhower said, when he took the decision to invade?' Tyler said, and a slow smile spread across his face.

'He said, 'Let's go,'' she answered, and she laughed and kissing and hugging him in a state of high excitement. 'I don't even know if it's possible at such short notice,' she said, 'but we could try, couldn't we?'

'I'll get you there, honey, if that's what you want. You wait and see.'

\* \* \*

That afternoon they had promised to visit Grandpa George. Emma had been putting it off because she was afraid her grandfather would say something blunt and unfortunate to her new man, but in the end Tyler said they shouldn't put it off any longer, especially if they hoped to dash off to France soon. Nothing was more important than family.

George's little sitting room had got a lot less tidy since Evelyn went.

'It's turning into a bachelor pad,' Emma whispered as she whisked away the wrappings from the fish and chips George had eaten last night. Then she scowled meaningfully at her grandfather when she encountered an empty beer bottle on the seat of the couch. He looked glum and put his pipe in his mouth.

'I see you like crosswords, sir?' Tyler said, in a bid to change the subject. He picked up the folded newspaper and was duly impressed. 'You've finished the whole entire thing!'

'Yes, I think it helps to keep me mentally alert. It's important to be alert,' George told him. 'Are you a pilot, boy?'

'No, sir, I don't get to fly myself. For every airman—or wo-man—in the sky, there are about a hundred staff on the ground you know.'

Emma smiled. *That's my Tyler*, she thought.

'Is that so?' George said, warming ever so slightly to the young man. 'At least you are in employment. I wouldn't want my granddaughter involved with some layabout.'

'No sir. I can assure you that I'm making decent money and my long term prospects look good.' Tyler answered as if he *expected* these kinds of questions.

'You've got a nice tidy haircut, too,' George mused. 'Not like that other fellow. What was his name, Emma?'

'I don't remember,' Emma said, and she gave Tyler another secret smile.

'Hey, sir, I was reading today about a crossword puzzle that came out just before the D-Day landings—apparently it caused one hell of a fuss,' Tyler said, and George pricked up his ears. 'The clue that started it all was *one of the United States—four letters.*'

'Well, there are only three states with four letters, to my knowledge—Iowa, Ohio, and Utah. I'd say if this has something to do with World War Two the answer must be Utah.'

'You got it, sir. Why, you are sharp as a tack! Utah was a codename for one of the beaches where our boys landed,' Tyler said, pleased that he had captured the old man's interest. 'But the clue that really got them worried was 'Red Indian on the Mis-souri—five across' and you know the answer to that too, don't you?'

'Omaha—the name of the other beach. And this appeared in the national newspaper, you say?'

'Yes. The powers that be got so worried about security, they hauled in the poor guy who set the crossword puzzle and inter-rogated him.'

'I'm not surprised—they must have thought he was passing information to the enemy.' George was leaning forward now, en-joying the conversation.

'But it turned out to be an innocent coincidence.'

'The poor man,' Emma said, 'he probably had a dreadful time convincing them of that!'

George chatted for a while, and he asked Tyler what he thought about this 'Red Indian' business with Susan. Tyler said he thought the family should be very proud. He said quite a few people back home in the States were finding out much the same thing, now that this type of DNA test was available. Emma smiled as she listened and did her granddad's washing up for him. Then Tyler said they had to go—they had arranged to call in at the travel agent.

'Where are you thinking of going?'

'Normandy. Tomorrow—if we can get a flight. We rang them this morning, and they said they'd do their best. Can we bring you anything back, sir?'

'I'd like some French cigarettes, please.' George said, ignoring the look Emma gave him. Then he lowered his voice, and leaned close to Tyler to make another request. He put a hand on the young man's arm, 'Do you think you could get me one of those sets of playing cards—you know—the ones with the *ladies* on them.'

Tyler's eyes went wide. 'I'll see what I can do, sir,' he said with a cough.

'I used to have a set, a long time ago. Evelyn must have thrown them out. You know the ones I mean, don't you, sonny? With the pictures of French girls in various poses—'

Tyler had not lost the ability to blush, that's for sure. 'I think I know the kind of thing, sir. I'll do my best.'

Emma rolled her eyes. Bachelor boys!

\* \* \*

It was all bad news at the travel agent. The flights were booked up. It did not look good. Tyler wondered if he'd been a fool to make that promise—about getting her there come hell or high water.

161

Emma tried to let him off the hook. 'I was being silly, Tyler. I had no idea that the anniversary was going to be such a big event this year.'

'It was bound to be, once the president said he was going,' Tyler said, ruefully.

'The president of the veterans' association?'

'No. The President of America.'

Emma gasped. Then she tried to pull herself together. 'We should stay at home and watch it on the telly, like normal people.'

'And miss the chance to track down Joe?'

They returned to the cottage in a bit of a gloom and Tyler spent the next hour on the phone trying to sort out another way to travel.

After scouring the Internet and considering routes involving Dover, the channel tunnel, or the ferry to Cherbourg, Tyler found a local airfield near Brighton, just along the coast. They flew small planes direct to Caen, in Normandy—and they took passengers, at a price. He rang them straightaway.

Emma was still desperately hoping to go. She acted as if it would all go ahead. She telephoned the school where she worked, and flapped round trying to get someone to do the Swim Squad on Sunday morning. She even started thinking about what to pack.

Keith and Susan were rather amused by all the frantic haste, but they weren't going to tell the youngsters not to try. Keith did ask his daughter if she really thought Tyler would be able to 'drop his responsibilities' at the base.

'He says he's owed a few days leave and he'll call in some favours,' Emma said, with absolute confidence.

Keith raised an eyebrow. 'I think that boy is genuinely fond of you, poppet.'

'I hope so, Daddy, I hope so.' She frowned. She didn't even like to think about how fond she was of Tyler. It had been odd today, at George's place, when she remembered that she had forgotten Matthew.

After yet another phone call, Tyler came back with a worried frown and a few sheets of paper covered in various scribblings. 'There's good news, and there's bad news,' he said, to prepare them for the verdict.

'Go on,' Susan said. 'I'd start with the good news, if I were you.'

'We can get flights to Normandy in time to meet this guy.'

The Rowlands all gave a cheer, in praise of his efforts.

'But,' Tyler began, looking up at three expectant faces, 'the first flight available is the morning of June 6th, the Anniversary itself. We won't be there in time for the memorial ceremony or anything. Everyone else wants to be there for that, you see, so the flights are booked solid.'

There was a pause. Then Emma spoke up.

'You know, that isn't important. Of course, if we'd had more time and planned this months ago we could have gone to that too, but really the purpose of us going to France is to talk to the veterans, and if we can do that, I'm happy. More than happy.'

Tyler gave her a grateful kiss, and Susan and Keith exchanged glances.

'So, we're going to France, baby, we're going to France!' Tyler twirled her around in his arms, enjoying her euphoria. It felt good to make her happy.

* * *

### June 6th 1944

Joe was on board the transport ship, sheltering from sheets of rain. They were crossing the channel at last.

'A little light reading, for you sir?' The soldier said. He handed Joe a pamphlet on 'What to expect in France'. It contained priceless gems of information about the place and its customs, and how to treat the local people—if any of them were left alive after the Allies had bombed the hell out of the towns along the French Coast.

Joe read it, for want of a diversion, although if anyone had asked him, he could have told them that boredom was not really a problem just now. The other men looked stricken with fear and trepidation, and the tension in the atmosphere was like a tightly wound piece of steel rope, straining and ready to snap. In that kind of situation, few activities seemed to have any real point to them, except maybe prayer.

The pamphlet gave a selection of French phrases that the powers that be had decided he might need. Joe smiled... somehow he didn't think that there would be much time for practising the parley voo when they hit the beach.

The guy next to him said he wished he could have got a letter to his girl. Joe said that was a shame, but he didn't know which was worse, to have to leave without saying goodbye, or to have to say goodbye and then leave.

'You went out with the blonde from the canteen, right?

'Yes, I did.' Joe said, and looked back in the direction of England, long since obscured by mist and rain.

His comrade in arms smiled, 'she was a firecracker that one. If Hitler had her on his side, we'd all be in trouble.'

'She sure was sweet when you got to know her.' Joe said, and for half a second a look of pride almost crossed his face, as if it was peacetime and they were having a beer after work. 'She's having a kid. We think it might be a little girl.'

Then they gave the order for the men to get into the landing craft, and issued them with their final instructions.

\* \* \*

Tyler went hurrying up the stairs to the men's dorm. He had to get changed and ready for work. Bradley was heading the other way and slapped him on the back.

'Hey Tyler! How's it going with Pocahontas?'

'Don't be a jerk, Brad.'

'You were with her all night again. Tell me, was she as wild as you hoped she'd be?'

'What?'

'I saw the way you looked at her that night at the dance. She's your fantasy, ain't she Tyler? She really lit your fire, didn't she? Dancing barefoot with her long hair flying out behind her. And that body of hers! You had to have some of that!'

Tyler grabbed his 'friend' by the lapels and shoved him back against the wall. 'Don't talk about her like that! Damn you, Bradley, I'll make sure you regret it if you talk like that again.'

'Ooh. *Damn you*. Strong words coming from you! I wonder what your bible-bashing folks would make of that.'

'Shut up! You low-down—'

'Listen! I've got a message for you! Your mother called up last night. To say your dad was taken sick.'

'Did she? Is there really something wrong with Dad? Or are you just playing some kind of dirty trick?'

'I'm not kidding. But don't panic. He's ok. She called back early this morning to say it wasn't serious. She didn't want you to worry. I said I'd tell you when you got back.'

Tyler released Bradley and stepped backwards, looking contrite. He hesitated. 'Did you say where I was?' he asked.

'Should I have told her you were at a prayer meeting? The kind that runs *all night*?' Bradley said, with a bit of a laugh.

A look of troubled uncertainty came over Tyler's face. 'What *did* you say?'

'I said you were on a training exercise.'

Tyler looked visibly relieved. He nodded, gratefully. 'Thank you. Thanks for saying that. It's not that I don't want to tell them —' He bowed his head. He was planning to tell them, it was hard to find the right moment, that's all.

'You don't want to upset them,' Bradley said, in a more reasonable tone. 'No need, is there, if it's just a fling?'

'It's not.'

'Then you've got a bit of explaining to do, haven't you?' Bradley looked at him, and gave a bit of a chuckle. 'I wonder what they'll make of your sweet little English rose!'

# 22

## Into the Blue Yonder

The tiny airport was something straight out of the 1930s. Its beautiful Art Deco building was gleaming white in the sunshine. It looked like the kind of place you should drive up to in a low sleek sports car. It would have been just perfect for an Agatha Christie story. Today it was crowded with tourists and holiday makers, off on a trip to France.

Emma and Tyler were in the departure lounge watching the comings and goings on the airfield. They had checked in their bags and they were just waiting for their boarding call.

'That could be our little plane, there,' Emma said.

Tyler glanced at it and ran a hand through his short dark hair. His eyebrows drew together in a worried frown.

'I do hope they remembered to do all their pre-flight checks, Emma. Do you think I should go and ask someone about it? I could tell them I'm a qualified mechanic.'

'No, of course not, silly.'

'Inappropriate?' he said, with a nervous smile.

'Definitely.'

He seemed jittery and odd. He went over to the water cooler again and got another cup of water. He fumbled in his pocket and found a small tube of tablets, several of which he dropped on the floor as he tried to get one out to swallow. 'Hay fever,' he said.

She wasn't convinced. He had never said anything about hay fever before. She knew him well enough to know he was lying. 'Tyler—you're not afraid of flying are you?'

'What me? Afraid of flying? No way! That would be a joke, huh—in the Air Force and to scared to fly! The guys in my dorm would have a field day if they heard that one.' He looked out at the little plane again, and rubbed his forehead, where beads of sweat were forming. He knew that small airplanes were more likely to crash than large ones.

The call for them to board was announced and Tyler clutched the chrome handrail in front of him.

'You are, aren't you?' Emma put a hand on his arm.

'No way, Emma! No.'

'I can feel you shaking, and you've gone all clammy. Tyler, for heaven's sake why didn't you say if you can't fly? We could have gone on the train or the ferry.'

'I said I'd get you there and this was the quickest way.'

'So you are admitting it, then, you *are* afraid?'

'Maybe just a bit. Not even afraid, exactly. I just get a little airsick.'

She shook her head at the ridiculous irony of it. 'Will you be alright?'

'Yes. I've taken a tablet, and I've said all my affirmations.'

She laughed. 'You are doing all this for me?'

'Yes,' he said. 'Yes I am, and it's worth it.'

'Have you got the boarding passes, or did you give them to me?'

'You've got them. Look sorry, I've just got to—' He ran off in the direction of the door marked 'Gentlemen'.

Emma had to loaf around the display outside the bookstore, waiting for him. She hoped he hadn't thought better of the whole idea.

* * *

***June 6th 1944***

Vera and Miranda watched from the attic window in the house on the headland. They could see an endless stream of vessels, a giant convoy heading out to sea. History being made.

'Did you ever see anything like that in your entire life?' Miranda said, as she looked down at the surreal scene.

'No, and I never will again. I hope not, anyway. Look at the sea—thick with them. Surely that's enough to knock out anything they've got over there. Surely.'

'They will prevail, Vera, they must, and then they'll be back and everyone will be so happy. Well, they ought to be happy, anyway.'

'You told your ma and pa about Ray yet? Did you tell them he wants to get hitched and take you back to Illinois?'

'I've got a letter written, but not yet posted. They'll have to know, if I'm to be his wife.'

'Don't post it,' Vera told her. 'Wait for news. Wait and see what happens. You may not have to tell them.'

'Don't say that! They're going to win, I just know it.'

'I didn't say they wouldn't win, girl. It's the price I'm worried about. The price of victory.'

* * *

Emma and Tyler walked out onto the tarmac now, hand in hand, the last passengers to leave the terminal. The plane was all poised and ready with its propellers running. The steward by the steps of the plane was waving at them to hurry up.

'I love you, Tyler.'

'Yeah, well, I'd say you know the reply to that. It's a whole new world being with you.'

'Come on, race me to the plane! Sometimes it's easier to do something if you just hurry up and do it!

'Don't let go of my hand, Emma.'

'Come on then!'

So they ran across the tarmac and climbed on board the plane.

When they were on board and buckling their seat belts Emma said she was curious about how on earth he coped with this problem at work. He explained that everything he had to do took place in the hangar, nice and safe on the ground.

'I've never had to fix a plane while it was in the air, sweetheart. They're easier to work on when they're stationary.'

When the plane took off Tyler went a most peculiar colour and he had made full use of his little paper bag.

The stewardess was kind. 'Are you in Europe for a holiday, sir?' she said, when she heard Tyler's accent.

'No. I'm stationed in the UK,' he said shakily, 'I'm in the Air Force.'

Emma smiled at the stewardess, who looked a little bemused. Just for once, Emma had an inkling that Tyler wasn't going to get the question about being a pilot. The stewardess told them to buzz for help if they needed it, and went to attend to her other duties.

'You must have to fly from time to time.' Emma said.

'Just occasionally, yes. If they require a mechanic for an exercise or something, then I have to go. It's rare though. So far, I think the worst thing I've had to do was make the trip from the States to the UK.'

'Yes—that's a long flight. How did you cope?'

'I took tablets, and I said a lot of affirmations.'

'Oh, Tyler!'

'I'm a really good mechanic.'

'I think you must be!' Emma assumed they'd have found a way to let him go if he wasn't useful. 'What if you ever have to work on an aircraft carrier, or something like that?'

'That would only be a problem if I got seasick as well, Emma! Maybe it's different.'

Tyler tried to look out of the window at the scenery far below them, but it only made it worse. 'I think the pills I used to take might have been a little more effective. These ones don't seem to be holding it at all.' He reached for another little paper bag. 'Sorry!' He was off again, and Emma just patted his back for him and told him it didn't matter.

'You do seem to be a bad case,' she said, 'What on earth possessed you to join the Air Force?'

'I wanted to find a bit of freedom, you know, from my folks —much as I love them. At the time I joined up, I would have done anything to be in that relaxed, free and easy environment. I couldn't stand another minute on the farm with Mom and Dad. Sounds terrible, but it's true.'

'You thought the Air Force would be relaxed and free and easy? Compared with life at home? Is that what you're saying?'

'Yep.'

'Oh, Tyler. Was it that bad?'

'No. It just sounds that way. I told you, I love my folks. I miss them really bad. Oh my, this is really bad. Really, really bad. The pills don't seem to have done any good at all.'

'But, Tyler, why the Air Force and not the Army or something?'

'They had an awesome recruitment video. Interactive. You pretend you're flying a plane,' he said, 'they really get you with that one. Like I said, it's the feeling of freedom, isn't it? That you can just fly away into the wild blue yonder. I liked that idea.'

The reality was rather different, however. Emma buzzed for the stewardess again.

# 23

## In a Foreign Field

They picked up a rental car and drove to the coast of France, with the windows down and fresh air streaming in. The plan was to meet up with the old timers and find out more. They headed for Colleville-sur-Mer. Tyler did the driving. He said it was nice to drive on the right again, just like back home.

'I'll be glad if Joe made it off the beach,' Emma said. 'I kind of wish that he survived and I hope he had some chance of happiness after the war. But if he did, it's such a terrible betrayal of Vera and my mother. That he didn't write to Vera and let her know. That he abandoned her, and my mum. I suppose lots of guys do that. They get what they want and then they go. The war just gave him the excuse.'

Tyler looked at her and took her hand. She wasn't sure what she saw in his eyes, she couldn't tell if it was tenderness or regret or guilt.

At the Normandy American cemetery, they went to the information desk, to explain that they were hoping to meet up with a party of veterans from America. The ceremony was very nearly over, and Emma wasn't all that sorry that they missed it. 'I think it would have made me too sad, Tyler. I'd rather think of him as he was when he was alive. The way he was in that photo of him and those other young lads, laughing and smiling, just before they left.'

There was a terrific bang which made them both jump, and then another and another.

'What in heaven's name is all that?' Emma said, and gripped Tyler's arm. It sounded like they were shelling the beach.

There was a young man with a clipboard, standing behind the desk. 'I believe they're firing a last salute.'

'Of course,' said Tyler, and nodded sagely. He felt a bit of a fool because he had practically leapt out of his skin when the gun went off.

'If you will come this way, I think I can reunite you with your party.' The man with the clipboard gestured them to walk with him. He escorted them down a wide gravel path between the white crosses.

They walked a long, long way, and they passed a lot of white crosses. The young official told them a few things about the cemetery as they walked. He explained that it was American soil, maintained by the American government. He told them that the graves were all carefully catalogued and marked with a row number, a plot number, and a grave number. 'So I can help you to locate the one you're looking for, if you can tell me the name.'

'That's what we're trying to find out,' Emma said. 'But I don't suppose we'll ever know.'

'Well, you see these ones in this area,' the guide stretched his hand out expansively. 'These ones are unknown soldiers. It's possible he may be here with them.'

Emma had to stop and look at the inscription on one of the unknown soldiers' graves. She read it out to Tyler: 'Here rests in honoured glory, a comrade in arms, known but to God.' Is that what happened to him, do you think?'

'Could be.'

'I hope he isn't here at all. I really hope he did see a little more of life.'

They caught up with the Vets on the headland overlooking Omaha Beach. They were a disparate band of old men. Some of them looked very frail now. They wore blazers and jackets and anoraks against the wind, even though the sun was shining. The rest of the crowd were beginning to disperse, but these old folks had to take things slowly.

Tyler introduced himself politely to the person who seemed to be in charge—'the Fuhrer', they called him, as a joke. He was a middle-aged man with sandy hair and a sad face. He gestured them to come and meet Vic, who had been in the same company of men as Joe. The rifle company.

'Vic Cooper,' he said, and he gave them a smile and a shaky salute. Tyler returned with a smart one.

'Such an honour to meet you, sir. Emma and I are just thrilled to meet someone who served in that brave company of men.'

Emma nodded at this, and shook the man's crabbed old hand.

'Yes. Less and less of us vets every year, son. I heard this morning that my old buddy John is gone; he was with us that day too. With him down, I reckon I might be 'the last man standing' so to speak.' He gave a wheezy laugh. Vic was in a wheelchair.

Tyler did the talking, and Vic said yes, a man named Joe was with them when they crossed the beach all right—everyone remembered that crazy guy who kept rushing back into the water. Well, actually, he supposed that only he remembered it now. He frowned. It was a sobering thought. However, he could tell them the rest of the story, if they had time to listen.

'Lots of time, sir, that's what we've come for—to see you, sir, and to hear your part of the story.'

'We were making an assault on a gun emplacement up beyond the beachhead. Up on the headland there. Big ugly concrete thing. We didn't know how many guys were in it, but they sure as hell were shooting like crazy. Anyway, we kept on trying to take it, and after about two hours they went quiet, and we waited, wondering if they were going to blow themselves up or something—or blow us up.

Then two men came out, one after the other, moving very slowly, and they waved the white flag—well not a flag, just some kinda white thing—a piece of sheet or something. But one of our guys, he was angry about what he'd seen on the beach and he just mowed them down...'

Emma looked out to sea. This was the kind of thing she was dreading. Awful war stories that sounded so terrible you couldn't believe people could be so bad. She didn't want to listen to this. It might not even be true. This funny old man could be completely confused or making it up. She knew she had to try to take it all in though. This fellow said he remembered Joe. They could always check up on the details later...

\* \* \*

### June 7ᵗʰ 1944

'You trigger happy bastard! What did you do that for, they were trying to surrender!'

The two men lay motionless on the grass. A fine dusting of sand blew across and landed on their bodies. Joe just stared and stared in shock and disbelief. It was hard to credit that people could be so bad.

The soldier who shot them was shaking with righteous anger and the need to vindicate himself. 'I don't think so somehow. How come there were only two of 'em? There must be more than that in there. They've been firing volley after volley of machine gun fire. What are the others all doing?' The young soldier looked scared half out of his mind. 'I'd say they are just tricking us. If we'd welcomed those guys with open arms, they'd have shot us all dead.'

Joe looked at him angrily. 'Haven't you ever learned, Orville, that you should always give your enemy some room to turn around.'

'Why?'

'So he can leave you in peace, you dumb ass. The most bitter fighting occurs when a warrior thinks he has to fight to the death.'

They sat there waiting to see what happened and it became clear that one of the German boys who had tried to surrender was still alive, they saw him trying to drag his twisted body along the ground to a place of safety. At first he did this in silence, but the pain got the better of him and he started to moan, and then to cry out for help.

'He's not injured so bad, that guy,' said Joe. 'I might be able to do something for him.'

'Leave him.'

'It's his leg and his arm, that's all, he don't need to die.'

'Leave him, Joe, he's not one of ours.'

'He's gonna bleed out, if no one helps him.'

'Yep, and you're gonna bleed out if you do help him.'

Joe turned and made his case to Bobby-Jim, who passed for their commanding officer since yesterday. Joe told him why he wanted to do this. 'If those guys up there saw me trying to help him—they'd know we'd accepted his surrender. They might do the same. It could do us all a favour. They won't shoot at me, not when I'm wearing this.' He tapped the front of his tin helmet, where there was a red cross painted inside a white circle. Bobby-Jim frowned and then he nodded and gave him the go ahead.

Joe went racing across the cliff top to help the injured man.

The young German soldier looked terrified when he saw one of the enemy approaching him. He made a pathetic attempt to reach for a gun.

'It's ok, I'm going to fix you up,' said Joe, and pointed to his armband, which also bore the symbol of the Red Cross.

'You are a doctor? Yes?'

'That's right, so you can take it easy now, old fella. I'm just going to do a field dressing.'

Joe put something under the injured man's head, and then he reached for his satchel and started getting out his rolls of bandages and his scissors and his bottles and stuff. He slit the man's clothing to look at his wounds.

Joe did what a lot of people who work in the medical profession do, he chatted on about other stuff as he worked, hoping that this would take his patient's mind off what was happening. As he spoke, he cleaned the debris out of the wound.

'You're a lucky guy, this ain't so bad. You'll be going home with a bit of limp that's all. You got a girl back home? I gotta girl, and she's waitin' for me. You got a *fraulein*, eh, soldier?'

Joe's pronunciation of the word 'fraulein' was so broad that the man didn't have the first idea what he was talking about. Joe got out a bottle of antiseptic. The man reached for it because he wanted a drink.

'No. No. You don't want to drink that stuff. Hey, I'll get you some water in a minute.'

'Water, water, yes.'

'Ok, ok. Have some water first, if that's what you need. Here.'

Joe reached for his water bottle and gave the man a drink. He glanced up at the gun emplacement, and noticed it was quiet. Maybe the guys in there really were ready to surrender. That would be good. Then he put the water away and found the bottle of antiseptic again. 'I'm going to put this on your leg, ok, and it's going to hurt, I won't lie to you about that. So I want you to think about your girl, your woman, ok? You know this word, woman?' Joe delineated curves in the air so the young man would know what he meant, and he tapped his forehead too. 'You think about your woman.'

Just a hint of a smile crossed the man's agonized face, as understanding dawned. 'I think about a woman. Yes.' He sighed and lay back and looked at the sky.

Joe administered the stuff and the young man let out a long yelp of pain.

'Good, good,' said Joe. 'Are you liking France? I always wanted to see France. I thought I might stroll along and see the Eiffel tour if our boys get to Paris.' Joe started winding the bandages neatly round the man's leg, making quick work of the field dressing. 'You been to the Moulin Rouge? Have you? I better not go there or my Vera will kill me.'

There was a sharp staccato cry. 'Get down! Get down!'

It was followed by machine gun fire. Joe threw himself down over his patient, and he never did see which side the bullets came from.

* * *

'What happened then, Vic?' Emma had got more and more involved in the story as it had unfolded, but Vic was quiet for a moment, looking out in the direction of Omaha beach. Tyler looked at her and shook his head, trying to tell her not to push the old soldier. It must be hard coming to this place.

'We had to move on to fight in Bayeaux after that,' Vic said. He bowed his head.

'Was the memorial ceremony very moving, sir?' Tyler asked, when he thought he saw tears in the old man's eyes.

'I'm glad it's over with, son, to tell you the truth. All that sad music, and hymns, and long speeches—and I mean *long*. Just Awful. One of them was in FRENCH, you know. These young fellows lying here, I don't think they'd have enjoyed it at all. I can't help but get to thinking they might rather have heard that old song about the Chattanooga choo choo. That's how I remember them. Young and full of life. I hope that doesn't strike you as sacrilegious. I don't mean no disrespect.'

'No. Coming from an old soldier like yourself, sir, I think you know 'em the best. You know, I think I can find that tune for you now, sir. My phone here links up to the Internet.' Tyler tapped something into his fancy phone/palm pilot thing that Emma was always teasing him about. He put the phone into the old man's hands and watched him beam from ear to ear as he heard the warm, lively melody of his favourite song.

Emma looked a bit worried but Tyler gave her a soothing look. All the mourners were dispersing now, and the music wasn't loud. It wouldn't offend anyone. Tyler waited by Vic's side while the old tune played out, and he waited as respectfully as if he was listening a lone bugle playing the last farewell on the headland.

'Vic. Do you remember Chief's real name?' Tyler said, at last.

'Of course, I do. Why?'

Emma knelt down by the wheelchair, and looked up at Vic. 'We think he might have been my grandfather.'

'So you are, child, you got that same look about you! Joe Casey's granddaughter, eh? Well, I'm pleased to meet you, sweetheart, I really am.'

Emma was ecstatic, and she kissed Vic on the cheek, much to his astonishment. She just couldn't help herself.

'We've found Joe, Tyler. You were right, then. He really was called Joe. Joe Casey!'

Vic invited them to join him and the other vets and their wives and relatives for dinner. They were all going out to a little French restaurant in the town.

'It's a real friendly little place, we go there every year. Long tables, lots of wine, lots of laughter. You'll like it.'

'We could, couldn't we Tyler? It would be nice to celebrate finding Joe.'

* * *

At the restaurant they decided against the snails. There were so many other tempting things on the menu that they didn't need to resort to that, however authentic it might be. Emma had the chicken in cognac, and Tyler had the filet mignon. They sat at a big long table full of people, and swapped stories about the war. Tyler got the pilot question a few times.

There was a man playing a squeezebox accordion to entertain the tourists, but he didn't stay very long. He was doing the rounds of all the restaurants that night. The group thanked him and gave him a good tip. They said they'd have to make their own entertainment. The wine was flowing freely and there was a lot of laughter.

Someone passed round a guitar and asked Tyler if he knew a party piece. To Emma's delight and astonishment, he accepted the guitar with grin and started to tune it up. It turned out that Tyler could play, although he was a little rusty. He strummed the strings, halting now and then. Each time he made a mistake he pulled a funny face and muttered an apology.

'You are full of surprises, aren't you Tyler?' Emma said to him affectionately.

'Yep. That would be me,' he gave himself a little musical flourish on the guitar.

'What songs do you know, Sonny Jim?' Vic asked.

'I only know the one,' said Tyler, 'well—it's the only one I can play right through to the end. It's about Idaho and everything it's famous for. Would that be okay—shall I sing it for you?'

'Is it about potatoes?' Vic said, and raised an impertinent eyebrow.

'It's got at least one potato in it, you will not be disappointed, sir!'

'Fire away, then!'

Tyler smiled and struck the opening chords, gaining confidence all the time. He sang a funny song with a country and western feel to it, all about the great potato state, and everyone listened and gave him a round of applause. Emma knew that she had never loved him more than she did that night, and she began to think about getting him back to the hotel, so that she could love him once again.

They brought the special coffees at last, and the evening drew to a close. Emma snuggled up close to Tyler and kissed his cheek. He nestled his arm around her.

'I don't want to put a dampener on things,' Tyler said, 'but I think we should confirm it with Vera. I'd hate to have got the wrong guy after all that, and she's the only one that really knows. With your permission, Emma, I'd like to ring her to-night.'

'Okay,' she said. 'You talk to her. You always said she likes American boys, and I'm beginning to see why.'

They said farewell to everyone in the group, standing outside the restaurant in the dark on that warm night in June. Tyler shook hands with everyone, and said a lot of elaborate thank-yous. When he came to say goodbye to Vic, he glanced about to make sure that Emma was out of earshot, and bent down to talk to the old man.

'Sir. Please don't take this the wrong way—I would hate to be rude after such a wonderful evening with you and your buddies, but I don't think you've told us all you know, have you?'

If ever there was a guilty look, it was the one that passed across Vic's face just then.

'I'll tell her tomorrow,' he said.

* * *

Back at the hotel, Tyler stood on the balcony to make his telephone call to Britain. The signal seemed to be better out there. Vera Fitchett's telephone rang and rang while she made her way up the hall to answer it. She wasn't so fast on her feet these days.

'Don't you ring off before I get there, whoever you are,' she muttered, as she struggled along the hallway.

She reached for the phone, and put it up to her ear. It was a bit of a shock to hear an American drawl coming down the line, especially as he said he was ringing from France. She put a hand on her heart, and said he had given her quite a start. Tyler apolo-gised for catching her off guard, and told her why he was ringing.

'I know you don't want to talk about it. That's why I'm only asking you to listen. You just tell me 'yes' or 'no'. Can you do that for me, Vera?'

Somehow, Vera had a feeling she could do anything for a man with a voice like that.

'We have done a lot of research, my girlfriend Emma and me. We don't think Joe died on the beach, even though we believe he may have been in the first wave of guys to land in France. It seems to us that Joe probably wasn't a combat soldier at all. Someone here has suggested that he might have been a medic.'

'Well, I could have told you that,' she said sharply.

'Yes, Vera. You *could* have told us that. It would have saved us a lot of time and effort if you had. Furthermore, I'll bet there are a whole lot of other things you could tell us. *Like his name.*'

'I can't, and I won't' she said angrily, and she sounded like a stubborn teenage girl all over again. However, she was older and wiser now, so she added an explanation: 'it's all I've got left of him. His name. His name that should have been mine.'

'I understand, Vera. I do. I can't tell you how my heart goes out to you, in your sorrow, in your loss. But my heart is also going out to my girl, who wants to sort this out for her mom, Susan. That's your Susan, and his. Don't you think Joe might have liked to have given his name to his child?'

Vera sighed. She was weakening. If Tyler had been there he would have dimpled at her for all he was worth at this point.

'Look, Vera. I know this is hard, so I want to make it easy. The people here have given me the name of a guy who was with those boys in the rifle company that day—working alongside Bobby-Jim and Orville. I've got my money on this one guy. I am going to say his name and all you have to do is say yes, or no. You have to tell me the truth now, Vera. *Promise me. That's what I need you to do for me today, Ok?*'

'Yes,' she said in a whisper, because she had heard the words before.

'Joseph Casey.'

There was a long, long silence.

'I knew I'd never see him again,' she said, 'I knew he was lying to me when he said he was coming back, bleeding vagabond. But the day you brought that girl here, the girl with the long black hair—I saw his smile. I couldn't believe it. She looks just like my Joe.' She let out a kind of laugh. A shrill, sad kind of laugh. 'I never thought I'd see that smile again.'

# 24

## Last Salute

Tyler told her that Vic had something else to tell them, and they called in at his hotel in the morning. Vic was waiting for them in the foyer, in his wheelchair.

'My daughter has gone to get some coffee,' he explained, and he asked Tyler and Emma to join him. They sat in the vestibule of the big hotel, and listened to what Vic had to tell them.

'Emma, my dear. Yesterday, you seemed so pleased to have found your grandfather at last, that I must confess I didn't want to give you any bad news.'

Emma swallowed, and nodded. Tyler took her hand.

'I have to tell you that Chief wasn't with us when we went on to Bayeaux.'

'Perhaps he was with the men who went to Caen?' she said, with absurd optimism. 'Or what about Cherbourg?'

'No, darling. He wasn't. We left him there, you see. Where he fell. The men who had been shooting at us from the gun emplacement, they surrendered, just like he hoped they would. A whole lot of them came out of there.'

'What about the German boy? The one that Joe tried to help?' Emma said, trying to make sense of it all.

'I don't know, he would have been buried somewhere else. I'm not sure what they did with their people.'

'So he died?'

'I think so. They were both lying there, and there was blood all over the bandages. We didn't even know whose blood it was. We had to move on. There were other people behind us who cleared up what was left behind. But Emma, I have thought about those boys often, between then and now, and I reckon they both had the same insane courage. One of them came forward to try to surrender. The other went out to accept it. It was nothing, in terms of the war of course, but I saw it as a little step toward peace, and we all wanted that—five years is a long time to fight.'

Tyler started thanking the man for everything he had said, while Emma sat there with her head in a daze.

'I just wanted you to know. You might want to lay a wreath or something. I wouldn't want to take that from you,' Vic said.

* * *

Emma wouldn't believe it. Not without real evidence. Tyler drove her straight back to the Visitor Centre, to get the guy there to look through his database, now that they had the name and they knew it was the right one.

'He didn't die. The Red Cross will have found him. They will have taken him away on a stretcher to a field hospital or something, and after that he got better,' Emma said, as they stood and waited at the enquiry desk.

'If he did die that day, he'll be on this database,' the young man told them, 'even if his body was returned to the USA, he'll be listed here.' The clerk had a sticker on his lapel saying 'Ask me. I like to help'.

Emma stood shifting from one foot to another, and she found herself saying, 'don't find him, please, don't find him,' very quietly, under her breath.

Tyler looked anxiously over the man's shoulder, at the long list of surnames beginning with 'C'. There seemed to be an awful lot of them.

'Did he have a middle name?' the clerk asked.

Tyler gave an impatient sigh. 'I'm afraid we don't know. It has taken us months to find out he was called Casey. Tell us we don't need his middle name as well! Whatever next, his blood group? Tribal affiliation?' Then Tyler realised how short-tempered he sounded and he started to apologise. 'I don't know what came over me. We're just anxious to know what happened. It's been a long search.'

'It's ok. A lot of people coming here get very emotional,' the clerk said. 'There are quite a few Caseys, I'm afraid. He was a private, you say?'

Tyler nodded.

'He's not there,' Emma insisted, and her face looked set and determined. 'He went on somewhere else.'

Tyler said nothing.

'Here he is.' The man had found the entry on his database. 'He's right here.'

A chill went straight through Emma.

Tyler squeezed her hand tightly. 'I'm sorry, baby.'

They were given a plot number and a row number and a grave number, and it took them a little while to find it. Emma saw it first, and she knelt down in front of the clean white cross. It looked quite serene, standing there in the morning sun.

Emma did what so many people do when they find the last resting place of their loved one. She reached out and she touched the letters that were etched there into the stone. She touched his name.

'Private Joseph O. Casey, 7th June, 1944.' She read it out loud. 'Oh, Tyler, He only lived for one more day—just one day after the invasion. He survived all that and then he only lived one more day! They shot him, they killed him.'

'It was a war, sweetheart, people got killed every day.'

Emma couldn't stop staring at the cross.

'He wanted to see France, and to visit Paris, that's what Vera told us,' Emma traced the letters of Joe's name with her fingers. 'And all he ever saw was that beach, and this headland. That was why he never wrote. All this time Vera thought he met another girl.'

'I think she knew, in her heart,' Tyler said, 'just like you and I did. But maybe she would have believed anything, rather than face the fact that he was gone.'

Emma looked at the inscription—*Joseph O. Casey*.

'What did the clerk say the 'O' stood for?' she said. Tyler looked at the slip of paper that he had been given, with the details on.

'Ohitekah.'

'That's very unusual,' Emma said, 'I've never heard that name before.'

'No. Neither have I. I'll look it up right now. It would be nice to know if it meant something.'

Emma wished she had flowers, all of a sudden, and she resolved to bring some tomorrow. She would bring lots, she decided, so she could put some on the unknown soldiers' graves, if that was allowed. That's where she would have laid her flowers if they hadn't found out his name.

'Here, look Emma. Ohitekeh. It's a Sioux name.'

'What does it mean?' she said, and looked up at Tyler.

'It means brave.'

*Brave.* That's when the tears came. They came and they fell and they fell right there in a field in France.

With tears streaming down her face, Emma stumbled toward Tyler and held him tight. 'Don't go to war, Tyler. Promise me you'll never go to war!'

He held her close, and he kissed her hair, but he did not speak.

# 25

## More

Things moved fast after they found out his name. The first person they wanted to tell was Emma's mother. They phoned her from the hotel.

'Mum, we've found him. He was called Joe Casey,'

'I know.'

'What?' That was definitely not the reply that Emma or Tyler had anticipated.

'You remember Bill from Maryland? He did a bit of sifting through his records and he talked to some people. Well, last night he rang me and told me the man's name was Joe Casey. He turned up some other stuff as well.'

Emma was flummoxed. Truly speechless. Eventually, though, she found something to say. Something relevant. 'Thank goodness it all lead to the same man. Vera confirmed it too, in the end.'

'But wait, there's more,' Susan said, sounding like a television commercial. 'I have a very interesting letter, and a photo, a nice one. He was a bit of a handsome hero, our Joe.'

'Not your average Joe, then?'

'No, definitely rather special. I can't wait to show you, Emma. If I was 'techno-savvy' or whatever they call it, I would scan it in and send it on to you in France—on the computer. Put Tyler on the line. Maybe he can talk me through it.'

Emma handed over the receiver.

'If it's already been sent to you electronically, Mrs Rowland, all you do is put our address on it and press send,' Tyler explained, with the patience of a saint.

'Do I?' Susan said, excitedly. 'I think even I could manage that!'

Tyler and Emma went and waited expectantly in front of the hotel printer. It was a little while before it whirred into action and spat out some paper.

There was a covering letter from a niece of Joe's, and a letter written by Joe himself. The niece said that her family treasured the letter because they had so few reminders of the man they all loved. The letter was not really for them, though. The letter was for Joe's sweetheart.

> My darling girl,
> I'll try to get the permission we need. I wish I could have sorted all this out before we had to leave, but you know how it was. I want you to know that when I got off the beach my first thoughts were for you. I was just so thankful I was spared so that when it's all over we can be together. Things are a bit of a mess here, no sign of my c.o. but as soon as he turns up I'll ask about leave. I heard that another guy in the platoon got compassionate leave to go get hitched, but that was before the balloon went up. I believe the circumstances were the same as ours. You tell anyone who asks that you are engaged and would have been a married woman by now if not for the invasion. It'll all turn out just fine.
> All my love,
> Joe.

Cody Young

'What does he mean, *I'll try to get the permission?*' Emma wanted to know.

'Permission to get married, I guess. I believe that a young man in his situation was supposed to get permission to marry from his commanding officer.'

'What the hell did his commanding officer have to do with it? Why did he need permission?' Emma didn't see the most obvious reason.

'He wasn't yet twenty-one, for a start,' Tyler pointed out.

Emma sighed. 'So young,' she said, and bit her lip.

'I read somewhere that permission was often required, and it wasn't always easy to get. You know, if a black soldier wanted to marry a white girl, his commanding officer could be quite difficult about it. Then there were some soldiers who went and fell in love with German girls. You can imagine how well that went down.

'About as well as doing the goose step for General Eisenhower, I should think,' Emma said, in a crisp tone of voice.

'Yeah. But you know how it is; Cupid never did worry about what anyone else was going to think. He just goes and shoots you with that bow and arrow of his. That's what happened the night I met you.'

The photograph came next; it took a few moments to print.

Emma picked it up eagerly. There was Joe. It was a much better one than the snapshot of him and his three buddies. This one was the classic portrait shot, taken in a studio before he left America. He was gazing out of the picture like a matinee idol, all young and smiley, with his chip bag hat at a jaunty angle. It was the kind of photo that you might see in a treasured family album, or standing on the mantel with a dusty old poppy tucked into the frame. He looked like a man you could easily fall in love with.

'What a shame Vera didn't get her letter,' Tyler said. 'It says here that it was sent back to his family, along with some other papers. They couldn't send it on to his girl because they didn't know her name. That's kinda ironic, isn't it?'

189

Emma felt a wave of sadness come over her again. 'We could take it to her, when we get back to England. She might like that. She ought to know he wanted her to be his bride.'

'I don't know,' said Tyler, 'what good will it do now?'

# 26

## Paris

They sat at a little table in a restaurant with a good view of the Eiffel Tower. Emma was holding Tyler's hand, and she wasn't crying any more, but you could see that she had cried a lot, these last few days.

'Emma, you know I won't always be in the Air Force.'

'No,' she said. She was looking across at the Eiffel Tower. It was misty and the tower was in soft-focus.

'But I will be for a while yet, and you'd have to understand that I could be sent on deployment anyplace and I'd just have to go.'

'I know.'

'I'm not sure if it's right to ask you to share all the uncertainty that goes with my job. It would be selfish, in a way, wouldn't it?'

'Mm.' She couldn't look at him. She knew what was coming. He was going home to America in September.

'But, I've come to a decision. I know we've only known each other a few months, but if this whole thing over Joe has taught me anything, it's that sometimes you have to act quick, or else something happens and you can be torn away from the person you love the most.'

'Poor Vera,' she said. 'It's such a shame she never got her letter. As soon as we get back home, we'll give her the letter, won't we?'

'Yes, of course. Baby, are you listening to me? This is important.'

The note of urgency in his voice surprised her.

'There isn't a war on, and I know some will say we should wait, but I don't know if I can hold off any longer,' he said.

She was looking at him now, and she could see he was tense. But then he got up, scraping his chair noisily, and some of the other customers looked up.

She finally realised what was happening when he went down on one knee. He took her hand in his, and his fingers were trembling. He looked up at her.

'Will you do me the honour of becoming my wife, Emma? It would make me so happy.'

At first, she wasn't able to speak.

'I know it's soon, but it's not too soon, is it?' Tyler asked her, with that diffident look in his hazel eyes that she had noticed when they first met.

'No. I mean, yes,' she said.

He smiled and kissed her hand. 'That's yes to me, and no to waiting, I hope?'

'Yes,' she said, stunned. 'I wasn't expecting this—'

'I know, I can tell,' he said, 'I just kinda wanted to spring it on you. But it's been in my mind for a while.'

'Really?' Emma couldn't quite believe it.

'Yes. I got you a ring, and everything.'

'Oh!'

'But, unfortunately, I'm going to have to get up now, because it's in my jacket pocket, over there. I guess I didn't plan that bit quite right!'

By the time he'd found the ring and sat back in his place at the table, Emma was blinking back tears.

'Did I do something wrong?' he said, in alarm.

'No, Tyler, this is such an amazing surprise, that's all. I suppose I was so busy thinking about the past that I didn't stop to consider the future.'

'Good,' he said, 'it's nice to be a step ahead, just this once. Usually I'm driving you mad and keeping you waiting. Now take a look at this ring I bought you, and see if you like it, because when I go back to the States in September, I want to take you with me.'

A worried look crossed Emma's face as she thought about all the changes they would need to face. 'It's a big decision. Are you sure that we're ready for this?'

He grinned at her. 'Are you a little scared of marriage, Emma? Like I was scared of sex?'

She blushed and smiled and told him he might be right.

'You'll be alright with me,' he said. 'You'll love it.'

He opened the little box to show her the ring, and the diamond sparkled with hope and happiness. There they sat in their own little world, making plans. Nobody was taking any notice now; proposals are not uncommon in Parisian restaurants. It was business as usual, except that a waiter came and offered to bring them champagne. Of course, Tyler said yes—hang the expense—this was once in a lifetime. Emma felt like the luckiest girl in the world.

'Did I ever tell you what the state motto is, for Idaho?' Tyler said, and he took her hand in his, and adjusted the brand new ring on her finger. It was a little loose.

'No.'

'It's *Let it Be Forever*,' he said.

'Is it really? That's lovely,' she said, 'really lovely.'

'Yes, it is. People don't always get forever, for one reason or another, but I really like the idea.'

\* \* \*

They went up to the top of the Eiffel Tower, despite the mist. It was damp up there and they couldn't see a thing—there was no view whatsoever—but they didn't care since they only had eyes for each other.

Emma was concerned that Tyler might not like the feeling of being up so high, but he said the fact that the tower was firmly fixed to the ground made all the difference.

There was a place to send postcards and they each wrote one to send to the other and posted them home to England.

Emma wrote this message on her card: 'Tyler, with all my love, you keep my feet on the ground!'

Tyler sent this one to her: 'To my sweetheart Emma, who makes my heart take flight.'

# 27

## Ooh La La!

Tyler sent a text message to his parents to say he'd phone when he could with some big news, but in the excitement of the proposal and talking about plans they forgot. They went wandering around Paris all day and then back to the hotel for 'activity'.

In the morning, at about seven am, Tyler's cell phone rang.

Emma went to answer it without even thinking, as Tyler was standing in front of the hand basin in the bathroom. He was shaving. Emma rather liked watching him doing that.

It was Tyler's mother on the phone.

'Oh, hello Mrs Robinson! Can he call you back in a couple of minutes? He's just getting dressed. No wait, here he is.'

Tyler appeared, towelling the shaving cream off his face. He looked stressed.

'Mom!'

'We got worried when you didn't phone. You said you had big news.'

'Yes, that's right. Great news.'

Emma could hear the shrill sound of the woman's voice as she asked her son some tough questions.

Tyler tried to take it all in his stride. 'No, I'm not at the base. We're in Paris, at the Boulevard Hotel,' he said. 'Yes. In France.'

'With some woman?' The voice was quite audible now.

Emma bit her lip.

'Well, yes I am. I'm with Emma, I wrote you all about her.'

'John!' The woman called out to her husband. 'Tyler says he's in France. In a hotel. With a woman.'

'Mom, let me explain,' he said. 'She's my fiancée—'

'Don't lie to me Tyler, just because you've been caught out. Of course she isn't your fiancée!'

'She is, I asked her yesterday and she said yes! I told you all about her, Mom.'

'You wrote me two lines! This is too sudden. We know practically nothing about this girl. I'm worried about you, Tyler. Have you been drinking?'

He sat down on the bed and listened to a stream of anxious reproaches. He rubbed a hand over his face as the tirade went on.

The woman with the shrill voice continued, trying to make sense of it all, which would have been a lot easier if she'd paused for a moment to listen. 'Tell me she isn't pregnant,' she demanded.

'She's not! Not yet, anyway.'

'Tyler, listen to the way you are talking! Have you lost all sense of decency? I just don't know what's happened to you over there! This woman seems to have led you right off the rails.'

'She's not like that—she teaches school,' he protested, as if being with a schoolmarm in a hotel in Paris would sound a little better.

Eventually Mrs Robinson seemed to have said her piece, and she wanted her husband to take the phone.

'Yes, yes. Ok,' Tyler said, 'Put Dad on the line. I love you too, Mom.' Tyler rolled his eyes. Emma sat on the edge of the bed, and tried not to bite her nails.

Contrary to her fears everything seemed to calm down a bit when Tyler was talking to his dad—although all she could hear was yes and no, mainly.

Tyler smiled in response to something his father said. 'Yes, she's pretty. Really pretty.' He looked up and his eyes met hers. 'That's right,' he said, 'I'm totally in love.'

Emma felt a stab of affection for him, along with all the anxiety.

'So you'll try to calm Mom down for me, will you?' Tyler said, and his father must have promised that he would. Then they said their goodbyes and rang off.

There was a bit of a silence in the hotel room.

'That went well,' he said ruefully, raising his eyebrows. Then he gave her an irresistible smile. 'It's ok. Don't worry. They'll get used to it.'

Emma wasn't convinced. All the happiness of their day in Paris, the day he asked her to marry him, it all seemed so transient and fragile. It might all dissolve into nothing. It could just crumble away. She felt as if she needed to struggle just to breathe.

'Emma. Calm down. It will be all right. Remember, I don't need their permission. I don't need anyone's permission, except for yours.'

She tried to smile back at him. Maybe it would all sort itself out. 'You've always had the go ahead from me, Tyler. All I ever wanted was the chance to say yes.'

Tyler pulled her down to sit beside him. He smiled at Emma, and he seemed skittish and flippant now that the hard part was over. It hadn't been so awful—breaking the news to his folks. Just because they were different—him and Emma—didn't mean they couldn't be happy. He stroked Emma's shoulder and tried to kiss her neck.

'Hey baby, you wanna play cowboys and Indians?' he said to her, with a slow, sexy grin.

'Tyler! That is a dreadful thing to say!'

'Oh, I'm sorry,' he said, and he blushed up fast. He looked very contrite. 'That was most... inappropriate.'

'Yes it was.' Emma tried to say it in her schoolteacher voice, but it was no good, she could not admonish him with any degree of sincerity. He was looking up at her with his warm hazel eyes. She melted and ended up back in the bed with him all over again.

# 28

## Afterglow

Everyone was thrilled to hear the news when they got back to England.

'So you reckon he is Mr Right, after all?' Helen said, when Emma had told her every detail of the day he popped the question.

'Of course he is. He's everything and more.'

'Get a grip, Emma. He's twenty-two going on forty, he's from a potato farm, he's got a funny accent and a prayer book in his top pocket. Plus he gets really, really, airsick. Are you absolutely sure about this?'

Emma nodded, blissfully happy. 'I can't live without him,' she said. 'You just wish it was you, that's all.'

Helen rolled her eyes. She said she hoped she was top of the bridesmaid list, and she wanted to know if 'liquor' would be permitted at the wedding?

Grandpa George was more enthusiastic about the match. 'Best not to muck about,' he said, 'although, the single life does have its compensations.' He was very pleased with his pack of saucy Parisian playing cards.

Keith and Susan were delighted, of course, although they did express some surprise about how sudden it all was, and they had their own private list of anxieties. Susan said she'd never thought a daughter of hers would end up being an air force wife. All that really mattered was Emma's happiness, though.

Keith insisted on speaking to Tyler, man to man. He wanted to try to make sure the boy meant what he said.

'You're quite young to be getting tied down,' Keith said, searching Tyler's face for second thoughts.

'Mr Rowland, being with Emma isn't being tied down,' Tyler said, his hazel eyes all ardent and sincere, 'it's freedom. It's independence. It's happiness. Everything a man could want, in fact. I know it's also a challenge—we are not so similar in lots of ways, but it's the life I want. I'll take such good care of her, sir.'

Keith reported back to Susan, and she said that love like that should have their full support. They went and hugged the young couple and said that they'd like to throw a party. It would be nice to sort of *cement things*, they said. Or if not that, to let the world know that love had got its way, again.

'The Robinsons could come over for it, if they wanted to. That would give everyone a chance to get to know one another,' Susan said. 'I'm sure they must be very anxious to meet Emma. And vice versa. I do hope we'll all get along.'

Emma had her doubts on that score, but she changed the subject. She wanted to know where Tyler's family were from before they settled in Idaho.

'My grandparents were from Wisconsin, I believe,' Tyler said.

'Where did they come from before Wisconsin?'

'I don't know, Ireland I think,' he shrugged his shoulders.

'Robinson doesn't sound like an Irish name.'

'Well I guess I'm a bit of a mixture, like most people.'

'There could be a story there.'

'Yeah,' he said, and he grinned, 'there's always a story.'

\* \* \*

They drove up to London to give Vera her letter from Joe—the letter that had waited sixty-five years to reach its destination.

They went into the little terraced house, through the dark corridor to Vera's little dining room at the back. The table was spread with a dark red cloth and Vera sat down to read her letter. She had to look carefully, to decipher the words, her sight wasn't what it once was, and the quality of the printout wasn't great.

They watched her read it, blinking back tears. Emma felt Tyler squeeze her hand. Vera was, as ever, very philosophical about it. She nodded and folded the letter up carefully.

'Always full of good intentions, was Joe. Don't make much difference now, does it?'

They noticed that she kept hold of her letter though, she held it against her chest, and she looked almost pensive for a moment.

Then, abruptly, Vera asked Emma to show her that engagement ring on her finger, so she could see if Tyler had coughed up for a decent sized stone. She seemed to be duly impressed. She sniffed and said it certainly looked like a real diamond. When she thought they weren't watching, she tucked her letter into the front of her dress.

'There wasn't any kind of trouble, was there, over you wanting to marry Emma?' Vera said to Tyler. 'I hope your parents didn't kick up a fuss.'

'No, Vera. It's a different world now. All sorts of couples get together.'

'They always did,' said Vera, 'but people weren't always very nice about it.'

'The Robinsons were wonderful,' Emma said, 'once they got used to the idea. Tyler's mum sent me a gorgeous patchwork quilt, a big double one—for my glory box. But it's so lovely I'd like to use it straight away.'

'Haven't you tried it out yet?' Vera said, with a sly look at Tyler.

Tyler smiled and put his arm around Emma. 'Anytime you want to, honey, I'd be happy to oblige.'

Vera laughed. 'He's come out of his shell a bit, hasn't he?'

They presented Vera with a photo album that Susan and Emma had put together, it was full of pictures of Susan as a child and at all different stages in her life, followed by some pictures of Emma growing up in Devon. All the moments Vera had missed because she had to give away Joe's baby.

Vera liked the one of Susan standing near the hospital, in her nurse's uniform. 'She's got proper qualifications, you say?'

'She was a nursing sister, yes. Very skilled.'

'He'd have been proud of that,' Vera said, remembering that Joe had no qualifications; he was hoping the war would be his lucky break.

'We are very proud of him too,' Emma said. 'We think of him as a hero, you know.'

They gave Vera a copy of the photograph of Joe, in a silver frame. She stood it on top of the piano. That was when the hanky finally came out. She hadn't seen him for such a long time. She said she'd tried to keep her promises to Joe. She looked at the handsome young face beaming out at her from the photograph, and she touched it as if she was stroking his cheek. 'I think you knew I'd always take care of myself,' she said, as if she was talking to Joe and he was standing right there in the room, 'but I sure wish you'd been here to do it for me.'

Tyler and Emma thought they should leave, to give her some time alone. Time to think about Joe. They were just about to go when a friend of Vera's called round to see her—she let herself in through the back door.

'Oh Vera,' she said, when she saw the new photo in its smart silver frame. 'Who is that nice-looking boy?'

'That was my first fiancé, in the war,' Vera said proudly. 'That was my Joe.'

'What a handsome hero he was. Very nice. I suppose he didn't come back?'

'No,' Vera said. 'He didn't come back.'

Then she picked up the album of pictures that Emma and Susan had put together for her, and put it into her elderly friend's hands.

'I do have some reminders of him, though, and they are very dear to me.'

Acceptance is a wonderful thing, Emma thought.

* * *

They decided to do a forties theme for the engagement party. It was Tyler's idea. 'After all,' he said, 'it was Joe and Vera brought us together.'

'But Tyler, I didn't have a clue that Joe even existed the night we met at the dance,' Emma said.

'No, I know. But it was the smile, you see. The minute I saw that sweet smile I knew I wanted to be with you—it reminded me of home. Vera says you get that from Joe.'

They hired the village hall for the engagement party, and everyone was invited: every Rowland they could think of, and all the other relatives. George and his cronies from The Willows. Helen and all her friends. Everyone on Tyler's crew at the air base, and lots of young guys from the men's dorm. A large selection of primary school teachers that Emma knew, and some that she hardly knew, most of them single. Jack Bovey, the local historian. The little girls from the Swim Squad, and their families. Even Bradley. He promised to be on his best behaviour, especially as the Robinsons were coming. Tyler gave him a long lecture about what would and would not count as inappropriate.

Mrs Edgecombe, the elderly midwife, had been quite surprised when she got an invitation. They sent it round with a box of chocolates, since her wager on the American soldier had turned out to be right. She said she'd like to come, but they'd have to keep an eye on George. He had turned into a bit of a rogue since he lost his poor wife. Almost a lothario. He had started to get a bit of a reputation at The Willows.

The village hall was crowded with people, all keen to start celebrating. There were lots of people from the dance class that Helen and Emma used to go to, so there was no shortage of people itching for a turn on the dance floor.

The guest of honour was Vera. She had been to the hairdresser to refresh her blonde curls.

'You look like a girl who knows how to tango,' George said, as they helped her into a chair near him.

'Don't be so cheeky, and don't try anything. I know your sort,' she said, and settled back to listen to the speeches.

Aunt Meg passed by, slightly tipsy already, going on about what a lovely fellow Tyler was. Ever so polite. 'Emma *was* going out with a chap in Manchester,' she said—to anyone who would listen, 'but of course, she was bound to turn her head when Tyler came along. After all, who wouldn't want to marry a pilot?'

Trust Auntie Meg to get the wrong end of the stick.

Helen took her over to meet Bradley, so he could explain his specialty to her.

Susan sat beside George, her adoptive father, and took his hand. 'You okay, Dad? You got everything you need?'

'Yes, love. Everything I need right here.' He put his other knobbly hand on top of hers. 'I suppose with all the fuss and bother over this party, Susie, you didn't have time to have a look at today's crossword?'

'Yes, I did, Dad. I solved it while I was waiting for the caterers to turn up. I got them all except for number nine across. I was hoping you could help me out.'

'That was the one I couldn't solve either, love. I was hoping you'd know.'

She smiled at him. 'You and Evelyn were my mum and dad, in the everyday sense of the word. But I did need to find Vera, you understand. I needed to know the truth.'

'I don't see what earthly difference it makes, really I don't,' Vera said, 'you are who you are.'

'Yes, I am,' said Susan, proudly. 'Did Keith tell you that we are planning a trip to America, so I can visit South Dakota? I'd like to get acquainted with my Native American heritage.'

'Is that what they call it these days?'

'Yes. I've got ideas for another talk for the Women's Institute upon my return, I thought about calling it 'The Day I Saw Red' or something like that.' Susan grinned. 'I did toy with the idea of changing my name to Siouxsie, like the girl in that rock band, Siouxsie and the Banshees, but maybe it's a bit late for that now!' She laughed and helped herself to another sausage roll.

A tray of champagne flutes, brimming with bubbles, appeared in front of Mr and Mrs Robinson, and the waiter urged them to help themselves. They both shook their heads and looked very disapproving. Keith gave Susan a worried glance. The Rowlands liked to enjoy themselves at a good party.

The gulf between the Rowlands and the Robinsons looked rather wide. In the days leading up to the engagement party, an uneasy understanding had been forged concerning the forthcoming marriage. Mrs Robinson had expressed her doubts about 'two people so different', but she said that Tyler was a grown man, and they were so proud of him—serving his country, doing his duty. They wanted him to be happy. If he had found someone he could love and commit himself to, they must accept it and be thankful. Keith and Susan agreed with that most heartily. They almost said amen.

When everyone else had been issued with a glass of champagne, Tyler got to his feet and banged a spoon against his glass to get everyone's attention.

'I'm so delighted to be standin' here with my lovely Emma right beside me,' he began. Keith was surprised at what a confident speaker the young man was, and he beamed across at the Robinsons, but they had both assumed a kind of reverential pose to watch their son say his piece. It was almost as if they were listening to an edifying reading.

'Being with Emma has helped me to understand a little about life, and love, and luck. I found out that some people only get to dance with their girl for a few sweet moments,' Tyler said, with a shy smile at Vera, 'while others are lucky enough to hold her for a lifetime, and grow old together. I don't know what my luck will be, I cannot know my future, but I am so glad that my sweetheart has agreed to take my hand and share my life with me. That's something to celebrate, isn't it? So, can we have some music please? Let's dance, everybody!'

The music began, and the sounds of the forties filled the room. The dancers weren't shy and they immediately started whirling across the floor. Tyler put his glass down on the table, and looked at Emma, the girl with the American smile.

'May I have the pleasure?' he said.

He held out his hand to her, and she took it.

Cody Young

Read an excerpt from Cody Young's new novella
*Scandal at the Farmhouse*

England, 1868

She was sitting on the grass overlooking the rolling English hillside enjoying the April sunshine, when Edward Allendale saw her for the first time.

He was walking across his meadow to inspect a stone wall that marked the southern boundary of his new farm. He was keen to see every corner of this fine piece of property that had fallen into his lap. He spotted the girl from quite a distance, for she wore a light blue gown. She did not see him approaching; she was engrossed in reading a letter.

'Hello there!' he said, and she looked up from the page she was studying, then pressed it to her chest, as if the girl feared him seeing what it contained. 'No, don't get up, lass. I can see you're busy with your reading.'

'Yes!' she agreed, clearly embarrassed. 'I'm sorry, do I trespass on your land? I used to come here as a child. It's such a beautiful place.' She smiled and introduced herself. 'I'm Clara Fraser-Hughes, from over there.'

She nodded in the direction of the big house, further up the valley – its big sandstone façade warm and impressive in the morning sun. 'And you are Mr Allendale of whom there is so much gossip!'

'Aye, that would be me.' Ned liked her informality and her youthful, friendly manner. He felt instantly at ease, and surprised himself by sitting down beside her. 'Do I encounter a friendly native at last?'

'You do,' she said, offering him her ungloved hand to shake, which he accepted warmly.

He grinned. She was so matter-of-fact, so direct. The casual greeting was improper by anybody's standards, and it excited him. 'Pleased to meet you, Miss Clara, I'm Ned,' he said, deliberately choosing to use his first name and hers.

He watched her colour up as he gave her an appraising glance. She was a fine lass – not exactly a beauty, but buxom and bright-eyed all the same. Curls of auburn hair escaped from the clasp that held her hair back, and she had a light dusting of freckles. Ned had always like freckles.

'Well, Ned,' she countered, speaking as if they were old mates meeting in a pub, 'what are you going to do with Laurel Farm? Old Cedric would have a fit if he knew it had gone to wrack and ruin!'

Ned was taken aback for a moment, by her words and by her manner. She spoke with a confidence that most people would find unseemly in a woman. He smiled. 'It'll be a place to be proud of in no time, don't you worry,' he said. 'I'm thinking of letting the dairy cattle go, and trying it out as a stud farm instead.'

'A bold plan,' she said admiringly, 'there's money to be made in fine bloodstock, that's for sure.'

That's what you are, he thought, the finest bloodstock I ever did see, sitting here on my land, as if you owned the lot!

Ned had not experienced such an immediate interest in a woman for quite a while. He felt a rush of excitement, a feeling of being truly alive on this fresh, breezy morning.

'It'll take hard work,' he told her, 'and I'll need to hire a few good men to help me, if I can work out where to find them.'

He frowned to himself, for it was not the pursuit of men that held his interest this morning. The way the breeze ruffled the frill on the front of her gown was very distracting. Ned tried to keep his gaze steady and on her face.

'You'll want to try the hiring fair in Hoxton,' she advised him. 'First Saturday of every month.'

She's full of surprises, Ned thought. She had just solved a problem that had vexed him no end. He raised his eyebrows for a moment and then he grinned. 'Oh aye? First Saturday of the month, eh? Thank you kindly, Miss Clara.'

He knew he should get up and leave her now, but he didn't go. If they were seen like this, sitting side by side, unchaperoned on the grass — tongues would wag. He should bid her good day, but he did not. Again his gaze fell on the gentle rise and fall of her bosom. He glanced at the papers she held in her hand.

'Is that a love letter ye have there?' he said, knowing full well that he was being much too forward.

'No! It is from my sister.'

'Your sister? And yet you blush and hold it so close!'

She laid the letter down on her lap as if to prove that it was not a billet-doux from an admirer.

Ned leaned dangerously close, pretending to look at the first page. 'Aye, well, maybe it is from a woman,' he said, and he let his fingers riffle the edges of the pages, 'for it is very long, and I doubt a man would find so much to say!'

That made her laugh, but the wind caught one of the pages, snatching it up in the breeze and blowing it away across the meadow.

'No!' she cried, and this time she leapt to her feet in alarm. 'I cannot lose it, for it contains much that would be seen as scandal!'

'I knew it,' Ned laughed, but he got up and chased after the letter for her. Being fleet of foot, he soon caught it and brought it back. For a moment he thought he should tease her a little more and threaten to read it, but her eyes looked scared now, so he handed it back to her without looking down at the writing. 'And you still tell me it's from your sister?'

Clara blushed. 'It is. She lives in Ireland. But she's not happy in her marriage.'

'Tell me no more, then, for there's nowt to be done for the poor woman.'

'It is a bleak lookout,' Clara agreed, 'but I still hope she will find a way out.'

'A woman cannot leave her husband,' he pointed out.

She was embarrassed, he could see it.

'My sister, Olivia – she believes that a woman's place in the world will change. Have you heard that there are politicians now who have raised the idea of giving women the vote?'

That explains a fair bit, thought Ned, the girl's a radical.

'I have not yet enjoyed the privilege of voting myself,' he reminded her, with a rueful smile. Now that he owned a bit of land, though, things would be different. 'There'll be changes one day, Miss, but I doubt that you and I will live to see them.' He always preferred to speak his mind.

'I am glad I have not scandalised you completely, Mr Allendale.' Clara stuffed the letter into a deep pocket in her skirt. 'I must go home now, before I am missed.'

Ned was sorry to see her go. He stood and watched her walk purposefully across the meadow towards the grand house, until she was just a small figure in the distance. In that blue gown she wore, she seemed like a piece of the bright blue sky, fallen down to earth. A delectable sliver of heaven, sent down to torment single men like himself.

He felt a sudden impulse to chase after the girl, to catch her in his arms and whirl her around, to lay her down in the long grass and press his mouth on hers, to let his hands roam under her sky-blue skirts and look for heaven's delights.

Scandal at the Farmhouse is out now on Kindle and other electronic formats.

**Connect with me online:**

My blog: http://www.codyyoungblog.blogspot.com/
You can also find me on Goodreads, Twitter and Facebook.